Struggling to find his own sexuality in rural Maine, Clyde fears coming out and facing his older brother's rage. His feelings for his own brother confuse him and he tries to avoid it all by smoking pot and having anonymous sex with men at rest areas. Then he meets Evan. Clyde must find the strength in himself to stand on his own feet and become a man worthy of Evan's affections. (M/M)

Clyde laughed again. It felt strange to laugh, foreign. Like suddenly speaking a different language. It felt good though. "John is only twenty-five."

"See, he's ancient," Evan said, picked a piece of birch bark from the truck bed floor, twisted it around his fingers a moment. "I'm going to apologize to him when they come back. I know this job is temporary, but I don't want any hard feelings between us after the work is done." He pulled his knees up to his chest, hugged them.

He was wearing insulated coveralls that were a bit too short for him. The pant legs rode up, exposing his shins. His legs were very hairy, with curls of wiry black hair cascading over the tops of his socks. Clyde thought what it would be like to run his fingers through that hair, to feel it quickly ticking against his palm as his hands slid up over his shins, past the knees and into the warm grasp of his thighs. He wondered if the amount on his legs was any indication of the rest of his body. Was he covered? Would it be rough, scratchy or soft and downy like he imagined John's to be?

He could feel his body reacting to his imagination and he quickly covered his lap with the bag of chips, resting it in the V of his crotch. He wondered if Evan noticed because he began to smile at him.

Also recommended...

You may also enjoy these other ForbiddenFiction works:

Cigarette Burns by E.E. Grey
Maddox doesn't want to be around anyone unless it's his pack of cigarettes. Yet, when Rory, the cute guy from the bar, not-so-subtly hits on him, Maddox figures he can always smoke later. He has something else in mind his ex-boyfriend would not approve of in the least. (M/M)
http://forbiddenfiction.com/library/story/EEG-1.000043

Don't... by Jack L. Pyke
"*Don't... open me.*" Three simple words that tease Jack, taking him places from his dark past. For Jack, BDSM is a way to resist his worst impulses. Yet, the stranger calling himself The Unknown seeks to use that to seduce him. As Jack slips further down into the abyss, two men hold the power to save him. Will it be Gray, the Master who knows Jack's every secret? Or Jan, the first man to give Jack a reason to hope? With deadly ghosts coming out to play, Jack may lose everything, even his life. (M/M)
http://forbiddenfiction.com/library/story/JP2-1.000134

Bridging Obsession

P. L. Ripley

ForbiddenFiction
www.forbiddenfiction.com

an imprint of

Fantastic Fiction Publishing
www.fantasticfictionpublishing.com

BRIDGING OBSESSION
A Forbidden Fiction book

Fantastic Fiction Publishing
Hayward, California

© P. L. Ripley, 2014

CREDITS
Editor: James L. Wolf
Cover Design: Siolnatine
Cover Art: Lentolo at Dreamstime
Production Editor: Erika L Firanc
Proofreading: JhP323

SKU: PLR-000167-02 FFP
ISBN: 978-1-62234-158-0

Published in the United States of America

DISCLAIMER

This book is a work of fiction which contains explicit erotic content; it is intended for mature readers. Do not read this if it's not legal for you.

All the characters, locations and events herein are fictional. While elements of existing locations or historical characters or events may be used fictitiously, any resemblance to actual people, places or events is coincidental.

This story is not intended to be used as an instruction manual. It may contain descriptions of erotic acts that are immoral, illegal, or unsafe. Do not take the events in this story as proof of the plausibility or safety of any particular practice.

Contents

Chapter 1

In the Pines

Clyde was never one to openly disagree with his older brother John, even when John said something stupid, like now.

"I'm telling you, right he-ah having an African American in the White House is the end of this country. We might just as well sign everything over to those godless Muslims, or worse, the French."

John never said the 'N-word', but he could make African American sound just as vile. He didn't speak the words as much as spit them.

"Yeah," Clyde said, not really paying much attention anymore. He had learned a long time ago it was just easier to let him have his say than to argue with him. When John got cornered in an argument, which was easy to do, he started debating with his fists, and in that sort of argument Clyde could never win. John outweighed him by twenty-five pounds and he loved to fight. That was how Clyde had lost one of his front teeth: he had suggested John might be wrong on immigration. That maybe it wouldn't be a good idea to send anyone not born here back where they came from. That maybe this country was founded on immigration and.. POP! that was the end of the debate.

Of course John was deeply apologetic after. He begged Clyde to forgive him and even worked a few tears into the apology. Clyde, however, knew he was sincere. The harrowing regret in John's eyes was too shattering to be fake. Besides, John lacked the ability to pretend to be anything other than what he was. So Clyde just kept his mouth shut and felt lucky he still had one front tooth left.

They were sitting in John's truck in front of Millers General Store drinking beer and John was smoking a joint. It was their Saturday afternoon ritual. They worked half a day on Saturday cutting out whatever part of the forest they hadn't finished on Friday, then treated themselves to a few beers on their way home. John was one of many private contractors working for the paper mills; stripping the forests, clearing the land, then replanting trees so, hopefully, future generations could do the same thing. His business was small, just John and Clyde. It could be bigger, he could make a great deal of money, Clyde suspected, though John just did not have the know-how to do that. John knew how to physically work. He busted his ass most days, but to perform any mental task beyond adding single digit numbers or reading further than a fourth grade level was too much for him.

They often shared the joint, passing it back and forth in the truck cab, windows wide open so the stink wouldn't saturate the foam stuffing spilling from the cracked and torn seats. But today Clyde didn't feel like getting high. Pot made him horny and he didn't think he would have time to sneak off to the Route 2 rest area tonight to trade blow-jobs with whoever happened to be there.

It was Clyde's only sexual outlet. He was still in his teens for another year and six months, still too young to frequent the bars in Lewiston or down in Portland. Not that his old Ford Escort could get him there. He was lucky the piece of shit managed to get him to the rest area now and again. He wouldn't have the money to get to the city anyway. What little money he and John made went to the household expenses. Mamma hadn't been able to work for years and so Clyde managed to save enough for the occasional bag of weed and gas money so he could get his rocks off once a month.

He wanted to help John with the business. If they expanded a bit and got a bigger contract with the paper mill, hired a few more men permanently instead of the occasional short timer to deal with deadlines, they could work their way out of the financial hole they were in. Maybe Clyde could actually get a weekly paycheck big enough to afford his own place. But John wouldn't allow him to interfere in the business. Clyde was still a boy in his eyes. "This ain't none of your concern," John had told him when Clyde had suggested ways to increase their income. "I won't have some fucking snot-nosed kid telling me how to run my business." That was the end of the discussion and Clyde hadn't brought it up since.

Clyde kept his trips to Route 2 very secret. John hated gays more than Muslims and immigrants. "Those damned ho-mo-sexuals," he would say, emphasizing each syllable of the word, "are directly responsible for the moral decline of this country." John listened to talk radio a lot and repeated what he heard. John could make homosexual sound more vile than he could African American.

John was a bigot. That was the hard truth of it. Clyde knew this just as he knew the sky was blue, grass green and his small, close knit family of himself, John and Mamma were just a fraction of the enormous Chute clan of Western Maine. A sprawling group that had never, in hundreds of years, spread further than a twenty-five mile radius of this small town of Devon, Maine. Population 1,956 according to last year's town report. A town separated from the rest of the world not only by the wall of heavy, pined hills, but also by its citizen's desire for isolation. Devon's neighbors were small communities like itself: towns wary of strangers and cautious of each other.

It was the perfect town for Clyde. He was a wary man as well. He had lived here his entire life yet had no friends whatsoever. He could recall many of the people of Devon by name, but knew nothing more about them. And he didn't want to know about them. Clyde did not trust people, because Clyde had a secret.

John's bigotry was a hard thing for Clyde to take. John, his older brother, a man he loved and admired for as long as he could remember, was controlled by his own fears.

Prejudice, Clyde understood, was fear masquerading as something more heinous. Fear of the unknown, fear of the different.

This terrified him, because Clyde was different. He was as different from John, Mamma and nearly everyone he knew as a bat is different from a bird. His secret was his difference from his family and neighbors.

"You want to go to Sparky's tonight?" John asked.

Sparky's was a roadhouse John spent most Saturday nights at. Clyde had gone a few times, but there were too many fights and he often had to walk home after John hooked up with some woman or another.

"Naw. I think I'll just stay in and watch T.V."

"That's all you ever do," John said. "You stay in every Saturday night jerking off like that, you gonna go blind."

"I'll just do it 'till I need glasses," Clyde replied.

John laughed, nearly spitting his beer over the dash. "That's a good one Clydey-boy. You a funny guy. 'Do it 'till I need glasses.' I gotta use that one."

A car pulled up in front of the store. It was a Lexus, black with bright shining chrome rims. John stopped chuckling and watched the sleek, dark vehicle park between their cousin Bobby Chute's motorcycle and a pick-up older than John's. John's eyelids nearly closed as he glared at the vehicle, his face growing pale, mouth dropping open like the hinge in his jaw had sprung. It was the look of jealousy that had grown more familiar to Clyde as he had seen it on his brother's face more and more often as each year passed. It was a look that asked, "Why can't I have something like that? Why do I have to work so hard for so little?"

A man climbed out of the car. He was young — about John's age — with short cut blond hair and a face as pretty as a sunset. He was wearing shorts that showed off his golden tanned, muscular legs, and an Abercrombie and Fitch T-shirt. A company that John called Abercrombie and Fag. The guy in the Lexus was beautiful and Clyde watched him walk toward the store and felt his mind wander up next to the man.

Clyde's sex life might be sporadic, but his fantasies more than made up for it. Scenarios of sexual encounters filled his head during the mundane, day to day activities. Scenarios that he used later in the night as he lay in bed. His hands, working himself up, then off. The fantasies sometimes came hard and fast, overriding everything else going on in his head. The glimmer of a muscled arm in a sleeveless shirt, a pair of hairy, muscled legs, a few stray pubic hairs peeking out over the waist of low-slung jeans. Little nuances like these set his mind in gear and he was having trouble controlling the daydreams. He would sometimes snap out of the fantasies, slack-jawed, chainsaw buzzing in his hand, saliva pooling in the corners of his mouth. It was beginning to scare him.

"City boy," John grumbled. "Fuckirg faggot city boy."

"Hey," Clyde said turning John's attention away from the blond, away from the danger of another temper flare, "let's go home and get something to eat. Maybe going tc Sparky's will be fun tonight."

"You really want to go out tonight?" John replied, the excitement in his voice raising it a few octaves.

"Sure. I can always beat off later." Clyde grinned. "I'm gonna need some of that joint though."

John pulled the roach from the ashtray and handed it over. "Smoke up buddy, we gonna have fun tonight." He pulled the truck away from the store with a squeal of tires, pushing a cloud of dirt behind them. The blond turned and watched them go. Clyde smiled at the man as they left, the man scowled back.

When they got back to the trailer park, their mother was in front of the television watching cartoons and eating a bowl of ice cream. She was always eating something, that is why she couldn't leave home. She hadn't been able to fit through the door in almost a decade. "That you, boys?" she asked when they came in, turning her head as far as she could. The rolls of fat on the back of her neck mashing against one another.

"It's us, Mamma," Clyde said and went in to give her a kiss. Layers of grease and old sweat clung to her cheek and she smelled musty, like the beaten down recliner she sat in. She sniffed the air like a bloodhound.

"You boys been smoking pot again? I told you that God-damned hippie weed gonna get you in trouble someday. You just wait, it's gonna get ya'."

"It ain't gonna get us in no trouble," John argued. "If anything it's gonna keep us out of it."

"How you figure that?"

"It just is," he said.

John couldn't argue with their mother. She was the only person he wouldn't fight with, even when she said something he disagreed with he always backed down and dropped the subject as soon as possible.

"There's last night's pizza in the oven if you boys are hungry," Mamma said.

Clyde pulled the box from the oven, slid the pizza on a pan and set it back in. He turned to oven to 400 degrees and set the timer for twenty-five minutes. The microwave oven had died a few weeks ago. It still sat on the counter, the inside a thick sludge of dried-on butter, spaghetti sauce and other food-like substances that Clyde could not identify. Mamma hated to clean. The pile of dirty dishes flowing from the sink evidence of her lack of ambition. Clyde would occasionally give a half-hearted attempt at getting the kitchen in order, but when John and Mamma refused to pick up after themselves, well... Clyde just gave up trying. When the timer went off he pulled the pan from the oven and set the pizza on plates. Two pieces for John, one for himself.

John sat at the table, glanced at the two plates and asked, "You only having one?"

"There's only three left."

John pulled a knife from the sink, rinsed it off, cut a slice in half and dropped one side on Clyde's plate. "Eat up. You don't want to go out drinking on an empty stomach."

"Thanks."

They ate with Tom and Jerry playing on the television in the other room. "This is good warmed up. You're going to make someone a good wife one day." John laughed and tousled Clyde's hair.

"Funny."

When the pizza was gone John went to the bathroom to take a shower. Clyde sat with Mamma, listening to her breathing and watching television with her. She held the remote control in her hand like a scepter and flipped the channels so fast he couldn't tell what he was missing. She stopped on one of the religious channels the basic (very basic really, less than thirty channels but hey, it was only ten bucks a month) cable provided its small customer base. Brother Jim, a fat preacher with hair as tall as the pine trees Clyde and John cut down every day, screamed at the audience they were all going to hell if they didn't do what God, through him, commanded. They were all sinners and damned but if they would just send him ten or twenty dollars or whatever they could afford, they might find salvation.

"Amen, you god-damned asshole!" Mamma screamed. Mamma had a bible and even glanced through it once in a while. She believed in God, but didn't believe He was an ugly, angry monster Brother Jim and men like him claimed — perhaps hoped — Him to be.

John stepped into the living room wearing a new pair of jeans. Darlene, one of the women who frequented Sparky's as often as John did, had bought them for him in the hopes John would become her exclusive boyfriend. It wouldn't work and Clyde nearly told Darlene this, that she had wasted 120 bucks on a dream that will never come true, but he didn't want to dash her hopes. She would find out on her own eventually. John, of course, accepted the gift happily, not realizing they came with strings.

The jeans clung to his hips as though afraid of falling, clutching madly to the high, tight swell of his butt. The denim hugged his thighs, showing off the thick slabs of muscle in his powerful legs and Clyde's eyes were drawn — as the jeans were designed to do — to the bulge in his crotch. The thick roll of John's cock reached for his right hip, stretching out for the one spot on his body bone could be felt not covered in overworked muscle.

"Jesus Christ," Mamma blurted, "you wearing them jeans or fucking 'em."

Clyde laughed. He looked up at John's face and found a grin there as well. He was modeling the jeans for them and Mamma's exclamation was the approval he needed. The jeans were doing their job, showing him off.

Clyde let his eyes drift down to John's naked chest and belly. The rough-cut muscle carvings were softened by a thick weave of dark hair covering his torso. His nipples peeked out of the near black swirls like sweet fruit on a vine, ready to be plucked or tasted. Clyde saw in his imagination's eye, doing just that: pulling the puckered nipples, one at a time, into his mouth. He could feel the hard ridge on his tongue and taste the shower water on John's skin, still laced with the hint of Irish Spring. And his imagined self let out a small chuckle as John flinched when he brought his teeth together, delicately pinching the sensitive flesh.

In his head he buried his face in John's chest. It was warm there and he could smell, under the minty soap, the aromas of the forest. John always smelled of fresh cut wood. You couldn't spend as much time as he does out there amongst the thick oaks and pines without it becoming a part of you. John's heartbeat, a strong and regular thumping, lulled the daydream Clyde into a comfortable numbness and when John wrapped his arms around him, Clyde knew he was safe. This is what Darlene and half the women at Sparky's wanted. They knew John was a good man. Yes, he had his violent outbursts. Clyde's missing tooth was evidence enough of that, but those moments were rare ones.

"What do you think, Clyde?" Mamma asked, pulling Clyde from his daydream. "You think John's ever going to have kids wearing pants that tight?"

He looked up, his eyes met John's and he saw there, in his brother's pale hazel irises an angry questioning. John had seen Clyde taking him in, absorbing his body like a sponge sucking up water. He had seen the lusty wandering of Clyde's eyes over his chest, belly and crotch and he glared at Clyde as though he had actually felt the sharp nips Clyde's imagination had taken at his nipples, felt his younger brother's fingers running through the hair on his body. Beneath the anger though, Clyde saw fear in John's face. Whether it was fear *of* him, or *for* him, he wasn't quite sure.

Instead of answering Mamma's question, Clyde mumbled it was his turn to shower. He ran to his room, gathered the clothes he would wear out to Sparky's and locked himself behind the bathroom door. He leaned over the sink staring at himself in the mirror. *What the fuck is the matter with you?* he asked himself. He had been having these visions of John for years now. Had been fantasizing John not as brother and father-figure, but as a lover. He dreamed of John, not only when he was awake, but when he slept as well. The fantasy had spread its roots through his quick daytime imaginings and down into his subconscious.

Clyde stripped, showered, shaved and when he was dressed and presentable, stepped out of the bathroom. He hoped John wouldn't question him about what had just happened between them, that he would just let it go. Clyde couldn't come up with a viable lie to explain why he had been mesmerized by John's half naked body, or at least not one John would actually buy.

"Well, ain't you all spiffed up," John said when Clyde presented himself before John and Mamma. He was wearing khakis and a pale blue dress shirt buttoned nearly to the top. They were not only his best clothes, they were the only clothes he had not ruined from sweaty days working in the woods.

"Ayuh, that's my handsome boy," Mamma declared in her thick New England drawl and lifted her house dress a bit to scratch at her leg. Clyde noticed her leg was bright red from mid-shin down. There were also splotchy patches of purple along the backs of her calves. It was poor circulation and the last time she had been to a doctor, more than ten years ago, she had been warned that it could become life threatening if she didn't get some exercise. She hadn't taken the advice and hadn't been back to the doctor since.

"He sure is, Mamma," John said while reaching out to adjust Clyde's collar. He unfastened the top button of Clyde's shirt to reveal the thin pattern of hair that had been coming in on Clyde's chest. "Almost as handsome as his brother. Right, Clyde?"

"Right, John," Clyde replied. John had donned a black tee-shirt while Clyde had showered. It was tight around his chest, but it put emphasis on his strong pectoral muscles. The wariness had left John's eyes and when Clyde looked up at him, he saw nothing there but the amused admiration John usually had for him. Clyde was John's kid brother and John often looked on him in just that way, like Clyde was just a kid. Honestly, Clyde often felt that way about himself. Like he was not a boy but not quite a man either. He was trapped between the two worlds.

They headed for the door and Mamma rose to her feet, leaning on the walker frame that never left her side. "You boys be careful," she said. "You drive if he has too much," she told Clyde.

"I will, don't worry."

She followed them to the door and stopped as John and Clyde walked out to the truck. Mamma was wider than the narrow trailer doorway. She hadn't tried to leave home in more than a decade. It was doubtful she could even fit through the door, then of course she would have to maneuver down the three small steps to the ground. With the walker in tow and the fact she could not see her feet while standing, those three steps might as well be a thousand. Mamma waved good-bye to them from the doorway.

They went out to the truck, hopped in and headed for Sparky's Road House.

Though Clyde didn't know it, before the night was over he would find himself in bed with John.

And, by the end of the week, his secret would be out.

Chapter 2
Honky-Tonk

Sparky's was wild that night. A local band called "The Buzzsaws" was performing covers of Def Leopard and Aerosmith hits. The small honky-tonk bar was filled to capacity and the only thing louder than the redneck rock music, as Clyde thought of it, was the buzz of a hundred different conversations fighting to be heard.

The last time Clyde had been here he'd watched a man stabbed to death in front of the stage. He didn't know the guy or his assailant but heard it was a disagreement over a woman. Apparently the victim had been banging the other guy's girlfriend. It was a terrifying thing, to watch a person's life extinguished like that in front of him. He'd dreamed about it for weeks after, waking up in the darkness of his room, screaming, seeing the light fade from the man's eyes as the knife plunged over and over again into his chest. He hadn't been back here since and, looking around the crowded bar, wondered why he had agreed to come back.

John, that was why he had come here. John had asked and he had agreed because Clyde would do nearly anything to make his brother happy. Even come back to this shit hole that had given him nightmares.

They had come to Sparky's early enough to nab a table, but if they wanted to keep it one of them would have to stay with it during the evening. Which meant that Clyde would have to stay with it. John would be busy socializing. That was fine by Clyde. He didn't dance and the few people he actually knew here he didn't really like. These were John's people, his crowd. Clyde only came here to make John happy.

John was at the bar ordering a pitcher of beer for them to share and a couple of shots of whiskey for himself. Sparky's never checked I.D.s, or at least not Clyde's. John had been friends with the owner, Sparky LaChance, for as long as Clyde could remember; Sparky let certain things slide for his friends. Of course, if the place had ever been raided he would claim ignorance that minors were drinking here. There were only a handful of sheriffs to patrol the entire county so the odds of that happening were minimal.

A blond woman Clyde had never seen before was talking to John at the bar. She wore a skirt so short Clyde could see her pink panties each time she bent a little over the bar. John was laughing at something she said, then gently rested his hand on her bottom. She giggled and gently removed his hand, then set it on her breast. His fingers immediately began working at the flesh, digging in hard enough to leave marks. The woman laughed and John let his hand drop.

"Jesus Christ, look at that asshole," Clyde heard. He turned to the voice. It was Darlene. She pulled a chair from the table, sat and watched John with the blond woman. "I swear, he fucks anything that moves. He'd stick it in a pile of rocks if he thought there was a snake hidden in them."

Clyde laughed with surprise. Darlene had recently had a hair perm and her head was covered in tight, dark curls. She still smelled of ammonia. "So, how are you doing, cutey?" she asked.

"Good. I'm doing fine," Clyde replied. He had always liked Darlene, but kind of felt sorry for her. She was spending her youth pining for a man who wouldn't give her something she wanted: commitment. But then, Clyde was pining for the same man. He wanted something different from him — or at least he thought he did — but he was no more likely to receive what he wanted than Darlene was.

"You seeing anyone?" she asked.

"No. I'm busy working all the time and..."

"That motherfucker!" Darlene interrupted. John was whispering something in the blond's ear and she tipped her head back and laughed out loud at whatever he was saying. Clyde could hear her laugh, high pitched with a squeak curling off at the end, cut through the music and chatter of the place. It was an annoying laugh, he thought. It seemed fake, like she was forcing a semblance of humor to impress John. John's hand was busy under the blond's skirt. He was working at something in the front. This was what had set Darlene off. From where they were sitting it looked like John had his fingers inside the woman. He probably did.

"Hey," Darlene said to Clyde, "want to make him jealous? We can go out to my Monte. The back seat is kinda small, but we could have some fun in the front."

An immediate rush of heat rose up Clyde's neck and he felt it sear into his face. "I don't think... I mean, I... I can't," he stammered.

"Not your type, huh. Well, that's all right. How about her?" Darlene indicated a red-headed woman in shorts and a tube top that strained to hold itself together under the force of her large breasts. A thick spattering of rust-colored freckles covered her chest and arms. Clyde's eyes passed the redhead to a man leaning over the pool table about to take a shot with the cue. He wore a sleeveless shirt that showed off the tattoos running down his lean, muscled arms. An unlit cigarette hung from his bottom lip. The law prohibiting smoking in public places was one of the few rules Sparky actually enforced. He was rough-looking, tough and angry. He reminded Clyde of John.

Fucking hot, he thought.

Clyde looked back at Darlene. There was a thin sliver of a smile on her lips. She had seen where his eyes had taken him. "Do you like that one?" she asked.

Clyde swallowed, hard, and looked down at the table, not daring to meet her eyes. Afraid that if he did she would know the truth about him. "Hey, honey," she said softly, perhaps noticing how uncomfortable Clyde had become. "Whatever you're into, it's okay. As long as it's between two consenting adults, there's nothing to be ashamed of. Got me?" Darlene set her hand on his arm, the long press-on nails, painted a deep purple, shimmered against his well tanned skin. He pulled his arm away, sliding it out from under her hand and hugged it to his chest. Darlene gave him a curious look.

"Sorry," he said. "Personal space."

"It's okay, cutey. We all have to build our own bridges. You're just putting yours together a little slower than most."

Clyde nodded his head, not daring to speak. Afraid if he did, he would either admit to her that he was gay or start crying. And he would not cry. He would not show weakness, no matter how much he felt it inside. It's a difficult thing to realize something about yourself that others might find repulsive. Especially when that other person is your brother, the one you love most in the world. Even though Darlene could not be sure Clyde was attracted to other men, she had told him that he was not a bad person for doing so.

He wondered though, how accepting she would be if she discovered those desires were directed at his own brother. She would probably be as disturbed by the revelation as he himself often was.

John finished with the blond and carried the pitcher of beer with two frosted mugs to the table. He filled a mug, handed it to Clyde, then poured one for himself. "Hey Darlene." he said, taking the seat opposite her.

"Hey yourself," she grumbled. "You might want to go wash your hands. No telling where that whore has been."

"Well, she seemed fine to me. Smell," he said and shoved the finger that had been buried within the blond's skirt under Darlene's nose.

"Get that out of my face!" Darlene screamed, shoving his hand away.

John laughed and nudged Clyde with his elbow. "She acts like she ain't never smelled another woman's pussy before."

"Shut up, John, you idiot," Darlene grumbled.

The smile died from John's face. He turned his attention to her, his mouth a hard grimace, eyes cold, fierce. "What the fuck did you say to me?"

Darlene instantly realized her mistake. Of all the things that could set John off, and there were many, nothing worked faster than to question his intelligence. Words like *stupid* and *idiot* were like waving a red flag in front of a bull for John. "What the fuck did you say?" he asked again, rising from the table. His fists clenched, then relaxed, clenched, relaxed.

Darlene looked up at him, her face hard, terrified. Her mouth hung open. Clyde could see her dry tongue rasping over her lips while her eyes glistened with unshed tears. "John, she didn't mean it," Clyde said, feebly attempting to calm his brother. John could easily strike out at Darlene; he wouldn't care that he had hit her in the middle of a crowded bar with a hundred witnesses. If Clyde tried to protect her, if he got between Darlene and John's fists, then he would be punished just as severely as she. He would be just a minor obstacle that John would have to punch out of the way.

"I'm sorry, baby. I don't know what I was thinking. You know I don't think that about you. I don't know why I said it. Please forgive me, please," Darlene begged.

As suddenly as the rage took him, it disappeared. A smile stretched over John's face and the light, happy glimmer returned to his eyes. He sat, nodded his head at the beer before Clyde and said, nonchalantly, as though he had not just scared the shit out of Darlene and Clyde both, "Go slow with that. You only get two, remember."

"I know." Clyde lifted the mug. His hands were shaking, but he managed to get the glass to his mouth and take a sip anyway. It was cold and delicious and he felt his body relax the moment the beer slid down his throat. He looked over at Darlene. She was shivering as if she was cold, even though the hard press of a hundred bodies in the road house had the temperature hovering near eighty. Sparky had propped the door open, but all that did was let the insects in. A mosquito buzzed near Clyde's ear and he swatted it away. Clyde set his hand on Darlene's and nodded his head to her. "It's okay," the gesture said. She gave him a weak smile in return, then dabbed at her eyes with her other hand.

Clyde was allowed two beers, which meant John was going to get drunk tonight. John never drove while intoxicated. That was what had killed their father.

Dad had been on a night out with his friends from the mill. They had gathered at a little tavern in Lewiston. Clyde never found out exactly why they had chosen a place so far from home, but he had heard rumors that prostitutes frequented the place. He thought the stories were probably true. That would be a draw for his father. He never really knew the man, not like a boy should know his father, but he was only five when the accident happened. He thought his father would be drawn to the Lewiston bar with the ladies of the evening because everyone said John was just like him. John definitely would have gone.

Dad had attempted to drive home after an evening of drinking and who knows what else, probably getting a scorching case of herpes to bring home to Mamma. He'd never made it home though. His car was found by an early morning commuter. He had driven into the river. There were no skid marks or any indication he had attempted to stop or swerve. He had just driven right into the water. The car was standing nearly upright, nose in the thick mud of the Androscoggin River. The ass end of the car had pointed at the sky. It must have looked like some weird doorway to another world, Clyde thought. The tall, dark, oblong object hovering there in the water like the monolith in that Kubrick movie.

That was when Mamma had started eating. She had always been heavy, a little thick in the middle perhaps, the puffy beginnings of a second chin, but not fat. Not like now. In thirteen years she had gone from 180 pounds to just over 500. She was eating herself to death and there was nothing Clyde or John could do but watch. The poor circulation in her legs had discolored them to the red and mottled bruising that looked painful, but Mamma said they didn't bother her. Clyde knew that the color of her legs was proof that her heart was getting weak. She hadn't been to see a doctor in ten years, using their finances as an excuse not to go. They all had MaineCare, the state's low-income health insurance and it would pay for the visit, yet she still refused.

"Don't you worry there, Clyde. Mamma's gonna be 'round for quite some time," she had said when Clyde confessed how worried he was for her. He knew it wasn't true. She won't be around much longer if she didn't get help.

The roadhouse suddenly erupted in the excited squawks of a scuffle. Clyde looked up at the source of the noise and saw the handsome tattoo kid he had been admiring earlier standing his ground against a pissed off biker brandishing a knife nearly as long as Clyde's forearm. The kid held the pool cue in his hand like a baseball bat, swung it a few times at the biker's fist, attempting to knock the weapon free.

John looked over at the action. His eyes widened excitedly, his expression exactly like a kid's on Christmas morning. He jumped from the table and started towards the fight. His fists flexing and relaxing, pumping themselves into a frenzy. Clyde could hear a low, rumbling laughter rising from his brother's chest. This is why John loved this place. It wasn't just the booze or the women that drew him here. It was the nightly prospect of a good fight that kept him coming back.

Clyde grabbed John's arm before he moved too far from the table and into the chaos building at the pool table. "Please, John, don't," he said.

John glanced down at Clyde, looked over at the scuffle, back to Clyde again. Clyde could almost see the gears turning in John's head. He was working it out in his mind. Should he have fun and join in the fight, or stay at the table with Clyde and Darlene? Have a good time or take the responsible route?

The decision was made for him. Sparky put an end to the fight: he pulled out the only weapon he had on the premises, an old cattle prod he had bought at a farm auction just after the stabbing that nearly closed him down six months ago. It was a monstrous long pole with a fat metal ball on the end and when he fired it up, crazy blue electric arcs danced around the ball, letting everyone know he meant business. He pressed the ball against the biker's back and pulled on the trigger. The biker, a thickly muscled man with blond hair pulled back in a ponytail, immediately dropped to the wooden dance floor. A puddle of urine quickly formed under him. The band stopped playing and the entire road house grew quiet.

"That's enough, you dumb fucks!" Sparky bellowed, then everything went back to the way it was before. The band picked up where it had left off and the biker's friends helped him to his feet. Blond ponytail staggered to a table in the corner, grabbed a glass of beer and downed it, shook his head and was fine.

The dancers before the stage began bumping and grinding again. "Let's dance," Darlene said, jumping from her seat. She grabbed John's hand and pulled him to the small dance floor. Clyde watched them from their table, still nursing that first beer. John was a good dancer, moving across the floor with a grace that seemed out of character for him. He held onto Darlene's hips and ground his pelvis into her, grinding his crotch over her rear end, then turned her and did the same to the front. Clyde felt a twinge of jealousy, then blinked with shock. He should not be jealous. He was John's brother, not his lover. When they came back to the table, Clyde noticed John's cock had shifted down his right leg and had grown considerably.

When closing time came, John was all but passed out. Darlene helped Clyde get him out to the truck and into the passenger seat. Clyde stretched the seat belt around John, snapped the fastener to the lock, then gently closed the door. "Thanks for the help, Darlene," Clyde said.

"Not a problem. You know, he doesn't deserve you."

"Maybe. Maybe I don't deserve him."

"It's sad that you think that," Darlene said, then turned and shuffled over the dusty parking lot to her Monte Carlo. She climbed in and waved to Clyde as she drove off.

When Darlene was gone, Clyde realized John still had the truck keys. He opened the truck door and tried to fish them out of John's pocket, but the jeans were too tight. He would not have been able to pull a single strip of paper from the pocket, let alone the ring of keys. He unfastened the seat belt and pulled John from the truck, leaned him against the side and slid his hand into the pocket. John groggily opened one eye. It trained on Clyde, but didn't seem to focus on him. "Wha... doing?" John mumbled.

"I need to get the keys," Clyde said. He pushed his hand in further and felt the fat head of John's cock brush against his fingers.

John sucked in a deep rush of breath and his head dropped onto Clyde's shoulder. His lips found Clyde's ear and he let out a soft moan, sending an excited shiver up Clyde's spine.

Clyde found the keys, pulled them out, then maneuvered John back into the passenger seat. Once he was secured again, Clyde went around to the driver's side, started the truck on the third try, then drove home.

Twenty minutes later they were back in the trailer park. Clyde brought the truck to a shuddering stop in the driveway and cut the engine. He looked over at John snoring lightly, face pressed against the side window, mouth gaped open, dirty scruff of stubble on his jaw. He was handsome when he slept. Probably because his eyes were closed, hiding the anger that was usually in them and light snores fell from his mouth instead of the usual bullshit. Yeah, John could be a prick, but Clyde loved him.

Now, though, he had to get John into the trailer. He thought at first he would leave him in the truck. Let him sleep the rest of the night there. They were home and safe... but he couldn't do that. It would piss John off to wake up in the truck, but more importantly than that, Clyde needed John inside. He wouldn't feel right sleeping in his small but comfortable bed while John slept in the truck, either secured upright by the seatbelt or sprawled across the cracked and worn bench seat.

Besides, it wasn't like this was new territory for him. Carrying his brother to bed after a long night of drinking was becoming almost a ritual for them. He would just handle this the way he had managed it the many times before. He opened the passenger door, unhooked the belt and pulled John from the truck. Wrapping his arms around John, he half-carried, half-walked him to the trailer, directed him when to lift his leg for the three short steps up to the door, calling out, "Step... step... step." John followed his directions, but burped a sleepy protest each time Clyde called for him to lift his leg.

Mamma never locked the door when they went out. They never worried about anyone breaking in. What did they have to steal, anyway? An old television with one of the government issued digital converters and a sixty dollar DVD player from Walmart? Even the thieves had better stuff than this. He dragged John down the hall, turned him into his room and dropped him on the bed. John held onto Clyde as he fell onto the bed, pulling him down with him. Clyde struggled to get up. "John, at least let me get your shoes off you."

John released him and Clyde unlaced his shoes for him, then pulled them off. The warm stink of his sweaty feet filled Clyde's face. It was a harsh smell, but not unpleasant. Clyde thought. John sat up and struggled to get his shirt off. His eyes were still closed and he seemed to be drifting off again even as he worked to undress himself. Clyde helped him with the shirt, then unfastened John's far too tight jeans and pulled the fly down. He gripped the top of the jeans and pulled them down, dragging John's underwear with them. He was wearing the familiar cheap, white briefs.

Clyde laughed to himself. *Leave it to John to wear 120 dollar jeans with two dollar underwear*, he thought. John's cock lay across his hip, the thick foreskin still damp with sweat from his dance with Darlene. Clyde slid John's underwear back into place, covering him, when John grabbed his arms and pulled him onto the bed with him. Rather than fight, Clyde settled in. This is what he wanted anyway, to lie in bed with John. To feel his strong arms around him. Feel John's chest, thick with hair and muscles, press into his back. He felt safe, protected. Loved.

No matter what this looked like, Clyde thought, it was perfectly natural. They were simply brothers falling into bed together after a long night of drinking. *There's nothing sexual about this*, Clyde thought, even as he pulled off his own shirt to feel the heat of his brother, and pressed himself back into him. He felt John's cock begin to stiffen and felt it, through John's underwear and Clyde's jeans, rub against his ass. It seemed to be digging in, as though it wanted to chew its way through the denim. He pushed his hips back feeling the strength in John move through him. Clyde's own cock strained against his pants, threatening to burst out of the material. John pulled him closer, his mouth gently caressing Clyde's neck. *Completely innocent*, he thought as the warmth of John's breath ruffled the stray hairs, tickling his ear. "I love you, John," Clyde said, softly, so as not to wake his brother.

"I love you, Dar," John moaned. Clyde frowned a moment, then realized he probably meant Darlene. John had said that he loved her.

Clyde suddenly felt an overwhelming shame. He was where Darlene should be, in John's bed, with John's arms around her. He didn't belong here. This was his brother. It wasn't right what he was feeling, it wasn't natural. He lay in the bed with John's arms wrapped around him, John's body pressed against his, and tried to feel nothing. Tried to suppress the desires he had for his older brother, these awful, disgusting desires. But he failed. His erection kept him up through the night and each time John shifted his weight a bit, or moaned in his sleep, Clyde felt his heart race just a bit. Just enough to keep the blood flowing into his dick.

Finally, when the sun began to fill the small bedroom with its morning heat, telling Clyde that this day, just like the past week, was going to be a hot one, sleep came to him. He did not dream.

Chapter 3

Dreaming in the Woods

It was Monday morning. John and Clyde were in the truck long before the sun had managed to climb the hills to the east. They each had travel mugs filled with hot coffee, the emblem from the credit union Darlene worked for etched in red and gold letters on the sides. Clyde took his with four sugars and enough half and half to turn the black liquid white. John pulled out of the driveway, taking a left towards town, the opposite direction of their work site. "Where we going?" Clyde asked.

"We have to pick up something first," John replied, not elaborating.

When they got to town, John pulled the truck in the credit union parking lot. There was a truck already there, parked sideways across two clearly marked spaces. A big man sat behind the wheel, a thick black beard covered his face. John pulled his truck next to the other one and nodded his head at the bearded driver.

"Good morning. This is Clyde," John said, cocking his thumb at Clyde. "Dale and Evan."

The driver, Dale, nodded his head in greeting. Clyde leaned forward to see past him, to the passenger, Evan. There wasn't enough light yet for him to make Evan out very well, but he looked young. Evan gave Clyde a quick smile, nodded his head hello as Dale had. "You guys all geared up?" John asked.

"Ayuh, looking forward to it," Dale replied, giving a sideways smirk through the thick bush of facial hair.

"Just follow us then," John said, then slid the truck back into gear and pulled out of the parking lot. The other truck followed close behind.

"I hired them to help clear the lot," John told Clyde. "Henderson will give me a twenty percent bonus if it's done by the end of the month. Of course that will just cover the wages for these guys, but it puts me in good standing with the mill."

John didn't have to explain and Clyde was a little surprised he did. The business was John's and he wouldn't allow Clyde to interfere with it, or even make a suggestion how things might be better managed.

"Dale and Evan are brothers. They're Darlene's cousins or something. Some relation to her, anyway." John sipped his coffee and glanced into the rearview mirror every few minutes to make sure the other truck was still there. When they arrived at the work site, Clyde checked the gas and oil in the skidder, a big, tractor-like machine with a claw for moving felled trees extended out from its front on a long I-beam, and he officially introduced himself to the new men. Evan was about Clyde's age. He had a handsome smile that he flashed around constantly and a lazy eye that unnerved Clyde at first. It was weird, his looking at you and the trees behind you at the same time. As the day progressed, however, Clyde began to find the flaw endearing. It made him think that maybe the eye had taught Evan sympathy.

Devon, Maine was not known for its financial power. In fact, most of the people here could easily be called poor. But Clyde's family was more than poor, they were seen as near destitute even to the most impoverished families in town. Which of course made Clyde's years in school lonely. No one wanted to associate with the poor kid. He was mocked, ridiculed and friendless during his high school years. Nothing, he thought, brings people together like a common enemy.

When Clyde saw Evan's lazy eye he thought that maybe Evan understood what it was like to be the butt of other people's jokes. That perhaps he, like Clyde, had been ridiculed and teased and that perhaps this had taught him one of the most important characteristics a man can posses: humility.

Maybe this crazy eye would make Evan more accepting of other people's differences and he and Clyde could become friends. That maybe Clyde's abnormality, as John would call it, his attraction to other men, would not lessen his appeal of friendship for Evan.

Clyde needed a friend. He needed a friend like a man lost in the desert needs a drink of water. It was almost a life-or-death urge and he felt like he was dying without company. If he couldn't have a lover, and he didn't think he could — not now at least, not here — then he would like a friend.

It would be nice, he thought, *to have both in Evan.*

Beyond the lazy eye, or perhaps because of it, Clyde found Evan very attractive. There was that friendly smile shimmering from him, as welcoming as a fog-splitting shine from a lighthouse. The unruly mop of curly black hair that stuck out of his head in every direction possible, suggesting that when he woke that morning he had splashed some water on his face and called it good. It wasn't a slobbish look though, but indifferent.

Working in the woods is a tough job. Evan didn't really have the body for it, at least not yet. He was skinny, weak-muscled and because he hadn't really had a physical job before, Clyde decided, he seemed to tire easily. Yet, he kept up with the others just the same. And he did it all without complaint. But when nine o'clock came and John called for a break, Clyde could tell Evan was near beat for the day.

Clyde pulled the gallon jug of water he brought to work each day from the cab of John's truck and climbed in the back. Evan dragged his feet over to the truck, then pulled himself into the back with Clyde. He had a two liter bottle of Coke with him that he cracked open and guzzled a quarter of it in one drink. Clyde watched his Adam's apple bounce in his throat. "I think I should have brought some of that instead of soda," Evan said, indicating the jug Clyde was currently tipping up to his mouth. Clyde let the cool liquid flow down his throat, breaking up what felt like clods of sawdust in his mouth.

"You can have some of this, if you don't mind drinking after me," Clyde said, holding out the plastic jug.

"Am I going to catch anything?" Evan asked, smiling when he said it.

"Just a little trench mouth. Nothing to worry about," Clyde replied, keeping his face as emotionless as possible.

Evan stared at him a moment, then began laughing. "You're kidding, right?"

"Of course I'm kidding. I don't have trench mouth. Hoof and

mouth disease, maybe. But not trench mouth."

"You're weird." Evan laughed.

"Good weird or bad?"

"There's no such thing as bad weird," Evan said and gave Clyde's foot a little tap with his own. Clyde surprised himself by not pulling his foot back. He never even thought about retracting his leg. Usually Clyde avoided being touched; he hated the intimacy of a casual acquaintance invading his personal space. But it had seemed so natural, as though they had known each other for years instead of just a few hours. It felt nice.

John and Dale leaned against the truck, each downing their own drinks. Like Evan, Dale had a bottle of soda as well. They were discussing the newest scandal to hit Washington, both quoting, nearly word for word, exactly what Clyde had heard on the right wing talk radio station John listened to. Evan smiled at Clyde and rolled his eyes. Clyde shrugged his shoulders. *What you gonna do*, the movement suggested. *They might be full of shit, but they are our brothers.*

"Hey, Dale," Evan called out, "it's funny you hate this spying shit, but you were all for the Patriot Act."

John spun around, glared at Evan. "What the fuck you mean by that?"

"I'm just saying maybe it's not the fact we are being watched, but who's doing the watching."

"You think the Democrats are going to keep us safe?" John said, his face growing suddenly very red. The arteries in his neck pulsating in abrupt rage. "You think those fucking pussies will do anything with that information but bring Communism down on us?"

"Communism? What is this, 1956?" Evan laughed.

John came around the back of the truck, lifted one foot in the air and set it on the tailgate. His fists flexed and relaxed again and again. Clyde saw what was coming. Evan was about to be beaten and he didn't think Evan's brother Dale, though being a very large man, could do anything to prevent it. When John got mad he was like a blind, mindless gorilla. Unstoppable and often undeterred.

Clyde jumped to his feet and placed himself between John and Evan. "John," he said with his hands at his sides. He wasn't going to try to hold him back, not like he could have anyway. He simply placed himself between the two in hopes it would deter John from doing what they all knew he wanted to do.

"John?" Clyde repeated, a light lilt added to his voice this time. A questioning. *Don't do this John*, it said, *please*. He was standing in the truck bed not only protecting Evan, but John as well. If he went through with this and hit Evan, not only might he lose his contract with the paper mill if the administration discovered an employee, even a contracted one, was fighting on mill property, but also Evan could file assault charges. They were struggling financially as it was, but if this happened they would be ruined and probably homeless by the end of the year.

More than that, he liked Evan. In just the few short hours they had worked together, Clyde found himself very comfortable around him. He trusted Evan. It was not just because they shared political views or only Evan's breezy attitude, but a combination of them. These things also turned Clyde on with as much ferocity as these same things made John angry.

And he had let Evan touch him. It was just a casual brush of booted foot that would not have even registered to someone else. But for Clyde this was revolutionary. Evan had entered his personal space and Clyde didn't even realize it until several minutes after.

John glared at Evan, looked into Clyde's eyes and held his stance for a moment. His shoulders back, legs spread wide, fists flexing. Then suddenly he let his eyes drop and turned away. He jumped down from the truck bed and stepped into the brush for a moment. Clyde watched John's back, rigid with tension. He heard John softly counting. "One-one thousand, two-one thousand..."

John wasn't smiling when he returned, but Clyde could see the fire had died from his eyes.

Clyde huffed in relief and squatted down next to Evan. "What the hell was that about?" Evan asked, keeping his voice low as though John were a wild animal and any loud noises might startle him into another rage.

"He has anger problems. Are you alright?" Clyde whispered.

"Yeah."

John had made his way to the trees they had dropped that morning. The pines lie on the ground, large red X's splashed across the rough bark. They had fallen on an ant colony and the tiny black insects crawled over the trees in such large numbers, the pines almost looked like they were shivering. John looked up at them. "Clyde," he called and motioned him over. Clyde jumped from the truck and ran to his brother. "Dale and I are going to the next lot to clear out them pop-lahs we started last week. You and Evan strip the branches from these pines. After that, I want you to show him how to run the skiddah and get this wood loaded in the truck." He nodded his head to the logging truck parked at the entrance to the road. "The driver will be here at four and I don't expect him to have to wait. Got me?"

"Yes, John, and thank you for..."

"I know," John interrupted, "just get this work done."

"We will."

At noon, they broke for lunch. John and Dale were still in the other lot with the poplars and wouldn't be back until quitting time. They had taken Dale's truck. Evan had managed to grab his lunch cooler just before they had left, which was good because Clyde had only packed a pair of sandwiches and bag of Dorito's. He would have shared, of course, but would have been starving by six o'clock when they quit for the day.

"So, how long you been doing this? Cutting wood, I mean," Even asked, pulling the plastic wrap off a bologna sandwich.

"About five years. I worked with John when I could through high school, and for a year full time since graduating."

"This is tough work. I had a job at the paper mill, but with the cutbacks, well, last one hired first one fired, as they say." Evan fiercely devoured his sandwich, taking bites so large he seemed to have trouble chewing what was in his mouth. Clyde ate his peanut butter and jelly more leisurely.

"John gives us a half hour. You don't have to choke down your food," Clyde said.

"Sorry. I'm starving I guess. I don't think I've sweat as much in my entire life as I have today."

Clyde laughed. "You get used to it."

After eating, Clyde and Evan stretched out, backs leaning on the sides of the bed, legs parallel to one another so Evan's feet were in line with Clyde's right hip. "So, you think John is going to fire me? Because of this morning?" Evan asked.

"No. I thought he was going to pound the shit out of you though."

"Is he normally like that?"

"Like I said earlier, John has issues. He's a good guy, but if something sets him off, well, look out is all I can say. I was actually surprised he backed down today. I've never seen him do that before."

"Maybe he's mellowing. Old age does that."

Clyde laughed again. It felt strange to laugh, foreign. Like suddenly speaking a different language. It felt good though. "John is only twenty-five."

"See, he's ancient," Evan said, picked a piece of birch bark from the truck bed floor, twisted it around his fingers a moment. "I'm going to apologize to him when they come back. I know this job is temporary, but I don't want any hard feelings between us after the work is done." He pulled his knees up to his chest, hugged them.

He was wearing insulated coveralls that were a bit too short for him. The pant legs rode up, exposing his shins. His legs were very hairy, with curls of wiry black hair cascading over the tops of his socks. Clyde thought what it would be like to run his fingers through that hair, to feel it quickly ticking against his palm as his hands slid up over his shins, past the knees and into the warm grasp of his thighs. He wondered if the amount on his legs was any indication of the rest of his body. Was he covered? Would it be rough, scratchy or soft and downy like he imagined John's to be?

He could feel his body reacting to his imagination and he quickly covered his lap with the bag of chips, resting it in the V of his crotch. He wondered if Evan noticed because he began to smile at him.

"Do you smoke?" Evan asked.

"Cigarettes? No, but if you want one I..."

"No, I mean pot."

"Oh, yeah. Occasionally," Clyde said, but what he thought was, *every chance I get.*

"You wanna smoke one? I got a couple of joints right here," Evan

27

said and pulled a hard pack of Marlboro's from his pocket. He shook out a joint, lit it and handed it over to Clyde. They smoked it down to a roach that Evan snuffed out and dropped back in the cigarette pack. The comforting buzz surrounded Clyde, like being buried in feathers. It was soft and beautiful.

"I gotta piss," Evan said, slid off the tailgate, walked a couple of hundred feet away and turned his back to Clyde. The hot, wet splash of his emptying bladder echoed against the forest floor.

Clyde's overactive imagination took over then. He watched as Evan, who was not really Evan, but an Evan of his fantasy, shook his cock but didn't slip it back in his pants buried beneath the coveralls. He let it hang out, fat and uncircumcised. A thick fold of skin hung over the head. He hadn't pulled it back to piss and the rim of foreskin glistened with moisture.

Clyde stared while the imagined Evan shook the cock in his palm. It was stiffening, swelling like a cooked sausage. Clyde remembered the last time he had been at the Route 2 rest area, down on his knees before an older man with silver streaked hair. As he choked down the man's oversized cock, he had looked up into his face and seen the same look Evan now had on his: desire and painful desperation.

Clyde slid off the back of the truck, approached the Evan who wasn't really there, and gently took his cock in hand. It was warm and fat and still growing. He pushed back the foreskin and the raw stink of sex and piss hit him. He liked the smell. Evan smiled at him, that crazy eye off in the trees. Clyde moved in and kissed him. His mouth tasted like pot and bologna.

Evan's hand slid down between Clyde's legs. His fingers fumbled with the fly of Clyde's coveralls. Clyde pushed his hand away. In his fantasy, Clyde was a bottom. A groveling, pig bottom who was here to service, not to receive any pleasure except the satisfaction in the other's orgasm.

This is also the way he was in the real world, out at the Route 2 picnic area. He was there to please, not to be pleased. He serviced the men there, but felt he didn't deserve to be served in return.

The fantasy Clyde dropped to his knees, on the same spot of ground Evan had just pissed on (that dirty pig bottom), and put the piss stick in his mouth. The taste was harsh and brutal, a morning's worth of sweat and funk trapped there under the skin, but it excited him, enthralled him in its fantasy filth. He slid the pants down and ran his hands down Evan's hairy muscular legs, then up to the smooth, blemish-free buttocks. A fine mist of hair covered each cheek.

He buried his nose in the thick, sweaty, black bush. Evan began to swing his hips, his cock sliding deeper and deeper down Clyde's throat. He twirled his fingers through Clyde's hair and face fucked him, grinding his pelvis against Clyde's face.

"You like my cock? You like it down your throat don't you, you fucking cock-whore," Evan grunted, slamming harder and deeper until Clyde thought his nose was going to break.

He did love it. Evan was right about that. He loved the hot-as-iron pole ramming his throat. He loved the sweaty man-stink, that funk of exertion and hormones and piss. He loved those heavy, goose egg sized balls covered in thick, wiry black hair, bouncing off his throat. And when Evan came, which he did just moments later, Clyde loved the taste of his oily semen, something that was only true for him in fantasy.

Clyde swallowed and swallowed, his belly swelling from the massive amount of come. He held onto Evan's shaking legs, twining his fingers through the thick, black hair on the backs of his thighs.

With his balls completely drained, Evan pulled out, his cock slimy with come and saliva.

"You alright?" the real Evan asked, walking back from his quick pee break.

The daydream dissolved as quickly as it had come. Clyde looked up at Evan, then down at his own crotch where the Doritos bag hid his still raging erection. "Sorry, daydreaming," he said. "I guess it's time to get back to work."

"Okay, you gonna show me how to run that skidder?" Evan excitedly looked over at the machine. The cab was small, about the size of a short phone booth. "Is there enough room in that for the two of us? Am I going to have to sit on your lap?" he laughed.

Clyde could almost hear his erection let out a nervous, "Eeep."

Chapter 4
Picnic in the Dark

"Hey, I want to thank you for getting that truck loaded," John said. They were on their way home from the long day in the woods. Clyde was hot and sticky, just as he was every evening after work. He badly needed a shower. His armpits felt like they were stuck with old chewing gum and his back itched from the coat of salty, dried sweat.

"It had to be done, right?" Clyde replied.

"Evan worked the skidd-ah okay, I take it."

"Yeah. He caught on quick."

"Good. You guys got along?"

"Yeah," Clyde said, then wondered what was going on with John. When John and Dale came back from the poplar lot, Evan and Clyde had the truck loaded and were waiting for the driver to show up. He was supposed to be there at four, but was an hour late. While they were waiting on him, they were tuning their saws, tightening and oiling the chains, cleaning the sawdust from the grooves along the motor housing, getting them ready to use the next day.

The buzz Clyde had from the joint they had smoked after lunch had long since worn off. Usually he felt doggy coming down from a high, sluggish like he needed a nap, but he didn't feel that way this time. Perhaps Evan had some really good bud, or maybe it was the company that kept Clyde feeling so upbeat. While they worked they talked about the video games they liked to play—Clyde didn't have a gaming system, but he had played quite a bit at his cousin Fred's—and the movies they had recently seen. Occasionally politics made its way into the conversation: they were both very similar in their progressive leanings, but after the incident with John earlier in the day they moved their conversation quickly out of the political arena.

John had climbed out of Dale's truck and moved so quickly towards them, Clyde thought John was furious at Evan all over again and was about to make him pay for his outburst earlier. Clyde placed himself between them once again and prepared himself to be struck down. Instead, John stuck his hand out to Evan and said, "I want to apologize for what happened earlier. If I scared you, I'm sorry."

Clyde simply stood there, shocked, mouth hanging open like he was a simpleton. He had known John to apologize just once, when he knocked Clyde's front tooth out. He had performed kind gestures after saying or doing something bad — buying Clyde a beer, dancing with Darlene even though he claimed to hate it — but only that one time had Clyde heard his brother actually say that he was sorry for something he had done. Until now.

Evan took John's hand, shock it. "Thank you," he said, "but I'm the one who should apologize. You are passionate about this spying thing. I shouldn't have mocked you. It was childish. I'm sorry as well."

"Apology accepted," John said. He glanced at Clyde, then quickly averted his eyes. He seemed almost embarrassed caught being civilized. Clyde felt a rush of pride that moment. Pride for both his brother and his new friend, Evan.

Clyde wondered what John's real motivation was for the apology and, perhaps even stranger, why he hadn't pounded the shit out of Evan to begin with. Restraint was as rare for John as it was for a hog with a full trough. Why would he not do the one thing he was known for? Why didn't he give Evan a thrashing?

Is John trying to be a better person, Clyde wondered. *If he is, who is he doing it* for?

"You want something at the stoe-ah?" John drawled as they neared Miller's.

"Naw. I just need a shower."

When they got home Mamma was in the kitchen, leaning on her walker. She was in a sleeveless dress and her enormous upper arms jiggled and flapped like sheets on a clothesline. She had made a kettle of boxed macaroni and cheese with tuna and peas. It was one of her specialties.

31

Clyde showered, then sat down to eat. It was cold. He went to heat it in the microwave oven, then remembered it was broken. He added some pepper and ate it anyway.

"I'm going to Fred's," Clyde said after washing his plate and fork in the sink, then setting them in the plastic strainer to dry. The sink was full of dirty dishes and he knew he would have to wash them soon. They were starting to attract flies. John or Mamma wouldn't touch them, but it would have to wait until tomorrow.

Clyde ached and he knew it was time to visit the Route 2 rest area. The Evan fantasy that had worked its way through his head earlier was still tearing hell with his body. He had been struggling with a semi hard-on all afternoon and he needed to relieve it. The climax free jerk-off he had in the shower only made it worse. And he needed to touch a real person, not a fantasy. He needed real human contact.

John didn't like their cousin Fred, which was why Clyde used him as his destination when he went cruising. John said Fred was a leech, that he had convinced his own parents to buy him the small house he owned and that his parents, now in their seventies, were killing themselves working to pay the mortgage off.

It wasn't true, of course. Fred had bought and paid for his own house a year after getting his real estate brokers license and Fred was now paying off his parents' third mortgage on their home. If anyone was a victim in this situation, it was Fred. But John couldn't be convinced he was wrong in his assessment of their cousin. Clyde believed John was jealous.

John busted his hump every day and had nothing to show for it. Their trailer was hot in the summer and cold in the winter. The pipes froze every year. They had replaced the floor in the kitchen and bathroom twice in the last ten years and now there were soft spots in them again. He worked and worked and things just kept getting worse for them. While Fred seemed to breeze through life, selling overpriced houses to people who couldn't afford them and filling his own house with every toy imaginable. He had a four-wheel ATV, snowmobiles, a new truck every few years, a large screen television with a surround sound system and every movie one could think of on DVD or Blu-Ray.

Yes, John believed Fred was a leech because he wanted to believe it. That the only way a person could have so much was to gain it dishonestly. So, when Clyde wanted to go out, he said he was going to visit Fred because he knew John would not check on him. He wouldn't ask about Fred when Clyde returned and he never spoke to Fred when he happened to see him around town. Clyde never had to worry that the truth he *hadn't* visited Fred would come out.

Clyde didn't like doing this, though. He didn't like having to lie to John. But what could he do about it, he reasoned. Tell John the truth about where he went and what he did? Tell John that no, he wasn't at Fred's getting high and playing video games, but out at the little picnic area on Route 2, down on his knees, back against a tree with some fat, tourist's cock in his mouth?

He drove through town, up Main Street, took Route 26 and in less than an hour saw the picnic area on the downward slope of Piker's Hill.

The light was fading from the sky as he pulled into the narrow drive. Shadows filled in the spots not occupied by mottled sunlight, giving the small park a sensation of camouflage, as though the place were hiding from the rest of the world.

The drive was a large paved oval that took him around the picnic area, past the half dozen picnic tables shielded by shaky wooden roofs, then back out onto the main road.

The small island in the center of the drive had a few more picnic tables, a barbecue grill cemented into the ground. There was low, scrubby brush that seemed to attract the travelers' family dogs, aching for a piss. The only feature needing maintaining by the state were two outhouses. The cheap green plastic walls were dotted with graffiti and large fist-sized holes let anyone who happened to stroll past the back of the outhouses a crotch level view of whoever occupied the toilet.

Clyde drove around the oval, noting the parking spaces separated by bright white paint lines, were empty. He rounded the curve and found the same situation heading out of the park as coming in, empty. He was the only person here. If there happened to be an empty vehicle or lone motorcycle Clyde would know that its owner was either in one of the foul smelling outhouses, or somewhere along the walking trails in the thin forest surrounding the place, and there was the possibility he might get in on some action. But there were no other vehicles.

Clyde parked his Escort, slid out from behind the wheel and walked to the picnic table at the mouth of the main trail leading up into the steadily darkening woods. He sat on the table, over the carved sentiments of undying love (T.B. + A.D. 4-ever), his feet on the seat and waited for someone to show up. If there were others here, like the old men that brought their own lawn chairs because they were more comfortable than the picnic tables provided by the state, he would at least have someone to chat with while he waited for an arrival that met his sexual requirements. Namely, the requirements being, they had to be under fifty with a dick that stuck out further than their belly. Other than that the only other necessity was their willingness to dance the dance.

Once the sun had completely descended into the west and the woods surrounding the picnic area had grown as dark and foreboding as Hansel and Gretel's breadcrumb trail to the gingerbread house, Clyde began to think that he should just go home.

The picnic area had no street lights to guide weary travelers into its restful arms, like the highway rest stops had. There were no sodium arc lights, shimmering in their weird orange glow, over the small outhouses reassuring women and the occasional nervous man that they were safe here, no one was going to attack them in this place. The only light available was from the moon and the dim glow of the stars blanketing the sky over Clyde's head.

He should just go home, lock himself in his room and finish what he had started in the shower. Jerk-off until his dick became tired and flaccid and every dirty sock littering his bedroom floor became gummed with his labor. He should... then headlights strobed over the small park as a vehicle entered the drive.

Clyde's belly suddenly twisted nervously. This place was dark, dangerous. He could see just a few feet before him. If this car held another man like himself, a man on the make, he might have someone to dance with. Or at least a conversation. But if this was a car full of less friendly types; bashers, young men with a father-sized chip on their shoulders, he could be in very serious trouble.

It had happened before. He had listened to a group of the old men sitting out here in their lawn chairs, daily newspapers folded over their pale, bony knees, tell about incidents in the late eighties and early nineties. Incidents where men were clubbed with baseball bats and tire irons. Where young men, the same age as Clyde, lashed out with a self-righteous hatred and impudence seen only in boys this age. Where they broke arms, legs and rib bones, cracked skulls and gleefully spit and urinated on their victims. The accounts reminded Clyde of Nazi stormtroopers cleaning out the Jewish Ghettos, or the fervent rage of the Hitler Youth he had seen in flickering black and white films shown during history class in school.

He sat upright on the table. Back arched, head held high, attempting to seem bigger, less vulnerable. He shoved his hand in his pants pocket and pulled out his car keys, ready to make a run for it if things turned ugly.

The vehicle made the slow run around the oval, pulled in a parking spot a few spaces down from Clyde's Escort and Clyde heard the heavy THUNK of the transmission shifting out of gear and into Park. The motor cut off and began to tick as the oil settled back in the pan under the chassis and the engine cooled.

Clyde watched the car and waited for the occupant (*please let it be occupant and not occupants — plural usually means trouble*) to emerge. Minutes went by. Hours, it seemed. He began to suspect perhaps the driver pulled in to get a few minutes sleep before moving on to wherever he was going. Travelers did that occasionally here. Stop for a few hours to get a catnap rather than risk falling asleep behind the wheel or spending the money on a motel room.

Clyde thought about leaving, getting out before his worst fears were realized and a lynch mob climbed out of the car. Just make a run for it. Get to his car, jump inside and tear ass out of the park and on the road to home. He had the car keys in his hand and just stepped down from the table when the driver's side door to the vehicle opened.

The dim glow of the car's dome light illuminated the only occupant as he emerged. He looked tall, muscular standing next to his car, the pale sliver of moonlight giving Clyde just a silhouette of the man. He could make out the wide shoulders, tapering in a gradual slope to his waist. There seemed to be some extra pounds on the man. He didn't look fat, just a little comfortable. Like a man who had never truly been hungry, but had never wallowed in gluttony either. The man cleared his throat, sounding like a gunshot in the near silent park, then he began walking towards Clyde, his footsteps echoing off the pavement like the beat of an executioner's drum.

Clyde could feel his own pulse racing, thrumming through his head in time with the man's footsteps. Blood pressure rising as the flight or fight instinct began to build in him. It was now or never, he thought. Run or prepare for battle.

Chapter 5
Dancing in the Dark

"Good evening," the man said. His voice was deep, but gentle. Soothing, fatherly. Clyde immediately settled back onto the table. His pulse slowed to normal and the sweat that had been forming on his brow, dried in the cooling night air. The man was still a good thirty feet away, still time enough for Clyde to run, but the man didn't seem threatening. He seemed a man just looking for a little companionship: a partner to dance the dance with, the same thing Clyde was searching for.

He was black. African-American, as John would have spit, as though the politically correct language he seemed compelled to use fouled his mouth. The man's skin was the color of the sky over their heads; dark, shimmering with a light coat of the day's sweat. Beautiful.

"Hello," Clyde replied, encouraging the man to approach, which he did with a hint of trepidation. He was as nervous as Clyde, which meant he was not here for any other reason than to give (and take) a little pleasure. He was not here to hurt or intimidate. "Nice night, ain't it?"

"Yes, very nice." The man stepped closer and came within touching distance. He was older than Clyde, perhaps by as much as ten years, maybe more. He might even be thirty; it was hard to tell in the dark. He was handsome, though. Clyde could tell that easily enough. "My name is Oscar," he said and stuck out a muscular, dark arm. His palm was paler than the rest of his hand. Clyde took the hand, shook it and felt the hard callouses along the pads at the base of Oscar's fingers. He must work with his hands, just as Clyde did.

"I'm Clyde," he said, giving his real name, something he rarely did out here. "So, what brings you out on a night like this?" Clyde asked, taking the lead in the dance. The thinly veiled questions, the probing as they waltzed around and around, working their way to the aggressive Tango, or a gentle ballet. Whatever they agreed upon could be performed on the picnic table, against a tree or perhaps in one of their cars.

"Just out looking to meet a handsome friend. I'm glad I found you," the man said and took another step closer. His shins touched the seat of the picnic table, straddling the tips of Clyde's well-beaten boots. Clyde could smell the peppery scent of Oscar's skin. It smelled nice, comforting, like a rich beef stew bubbling away on the stove on a winter's evening.

"I'm glad you found me, too," Clyde said and before they could talk each other out of doing what they had come here to do, Clyde slid his hands between Oscar's legs. The firm knobs of Oscar's testicles filled Clyde's palm. He could feel each nut, firm but with a sponge-like give to them, and the leathery sack enclosing them through the thin sweatpants Oscar wore. Clyde squeezed, his grip tightened around Oscar's balls, not enough to hurt, but enough to let the other man know Clyde meant business. Oscar's face split into a mischievous grin.

"That feels good," Oscar cooed as he reached out and fondled Clyde between the legs. Clyde pushed Oscar's hand away. He didn't like to be touched, even when he had sex. Oscar gave him a confused look.

"Just let me play with you for a while," Clyde said. Oscar smiled, pulled his hands back, let Clyde have his fun.

Clyde set his car keys on the table, then moved his fingers up, above the scrotum, to the root of Oscar's cock and traced the length. It seemed to stretch forever down into the baggy right pant leg. He finally found the head and gave it a little pinch with his fingertips, feeling the tight foreskin shiver over the glans. He grabbed the waist of Oscar's sweatpants and pulled them down. The fat, musky cock jumped from the thatch of thin, neatly trimmed curls of dark hair and he marveled at how wonderfully dark the skin was. Almost as dark as the night surrounding it. Clyde saw a pearl of glistening moisture at the piss-slit, winking out through the puckered ridge of foreskin. He pushed the skin back, revealing the lighter colored head. He lapped the drop of fluid onto his tongue. It was slick, greasy and just the lightest hint of sweetness.

Oscar moaned in appreciation, lifted his hands like he wanted to touch Clyde again, then dropped them to his sides and let Clyde do what he wanted to do. Because what Clyde wanted was what Oscar wanted. The dance.

Clyde slid from the picnic table down to the seat he had been resting his feet on and dipped his head down to taste the warm, black balls he had touched with his fingertips. He pulled each one into his mouth, one at a time, and felt the flesh of Oscar's scrotum settle into the space where his front tooth had once been. The salty tang of sweat and the shivery delight of hormones wrapped around his head like a turban, enveloping him in the wonderful smells and flavors of sex. Clyde's entire body quivered at the feel of the large, black cock rubbing against his face. He inhaled deeply, absorbing the smells of the crotch that had not felt soap and water since that morning and the faint traces of the piss that had been expelled since Oscar last showered. He worked each testicle, feeling them bounce over his tongue and move around his mouth like one of those everlasting gobstoppers he used to get at Miller's General Store when he was a kid. Then, he let Oscar's balls leave his mouth with a wet PLOP. The hair on the scrotum wet and clumped in downward pointing tangles, like stalagmites in a cave.

He opened wide and pulled the fat, black cock into his mouth. "Oh Jesus, boy." Oscar whispered as though this place was a sanctuary, a cathedral instead of a quick stop for a weary traveler to rest a moment or take a much needed shit. Perhaps, it was a church of sorts for him. Much as it was for Clyde. A place Oscar could be himself, without the cold, questioning eyes of family, friends and, more likely than not, wife.

After all, most of the men who frequented this place were married. Clyde knew this. He knew that nothing meaningful could come from the casual associations here. Knew that although they had fun, most of the men wouldn't even look him in the eye if he happened to meet them on the street. That, however, was a safety of its own. He didn't have to worry that one of his dance partners would confront him elsewhere, forcing John to ask how he knew this man. Clyde was as much in the closet as the married men he sucked off in the dark.

Clyde rolled his tongue over the head, curling it around the edge of the mushroom tip, then flattened his tongue to a hard plane which he pressed against the underside of the cock as he pushed himself down on it again.

"You like that, don't you?" Oscar grunted. "You like that big..." and here Oscar said something that shocked Clyde. It was a word so vulgar that even a man as angry and bigoted as John would not utter, the N-word.

Oscar said it though. He said it and he wanted Clyde to repeat it. "You like that nigger dick, don't you?" He leaned in, forcing more of himself down Clyde's throat and said it again. "You like that nigger dick. Say it. Say you like that nigger dick."

But Clyde wouldn't say it. He wasn't afraid of offending Oscar, the only black man he had ever really met, and the first he had been with. Oscar obviously wasn't offended by the word, but Clyde couldn't do it. He couldn't cross that line.

Instead, Clyde pulled open his own pants and freed his erection. He tugged on himself while Oscar pumped his hips, shoving himself further and further down Clyde's throat, toying with the gag reflex that filled Clyde's mouth with fresh saliva. Clyde could feel Oscar's cock grow even more rigid until it felt as strong as steel. It flexed and throbbed and Clyde knew that Oscar could not hold on much longer.

He pulled on himself harder, wanting to reach orgasm when Oscar did. He wanted to feel the rush of his own seed leaving him down below, as Oscar's seed filled him above. He wanted savor his first taste of a black man's semen. *Does it taste like a white man's?* he wondered.

In less than a minute after he thought the question, he found out. It did taste like a white man's semen. It was bitter with a mild, sweet aftertaste, just like every other man he had tasted. His own orgasm came a moment after Oscar's. It came with such a force, he nearly pitched forward, nearly rammed the last few inches of Oscar's massive cock down his throat. Come littered the grass between Oscar's feet, spraying several feet out, across the lawn until it met with the base of an old oak guarding the path entrance to the woods.

Clyde pulled himself free of Oscar's quickly softening cock, turned, leaned over the top of the table and spit the oily wad of semen into the grass. He shoved himself back into his pants, turned back to Oscar, who was pulling his sweatpants back up over his slightly husky hips, and picked up his car keys he had set on the table when the dance began.

"Well, that was incredible," Oscar said. "You sure do know what you're doing."

"I try," Clyde said, smiling. "I'm sorry I didn't, um... say that word you wanted me to say."

"What word is that?" Oscar replied, his brow furrowing in visible confusion.

"You know, the N-word. I just can't bring myself to say it."

"Oh," Oscar said, his head dropping slightly. "I use that word too much. But, I guess it's different for me, isn't it?"

"I guess. Yeah, it probably is."

"Look, you are a good man, uh... Clyde, right? Yeah, you are a good man for not saying that word even though a black man wanted you to say it. You are a good man for standing with your principals and not backing down even though the only person that would have heard you, is me. And I didn't give a shit if you said the word. I requested you to say it. But you didn't. Your Daddy must be a proud man. He did a fine job raising you."

"Actually, my brother raised me."

"Then he is a good brother. He must be a good man," he said and pressed a button on the side of his watch. It glowed a florescent green, showing him the time. "I have to go, but this was fun. Maybe I'll see you around again sometime."

"Yeah, that would be cool," Clyde said, but he knew the chances of them ever meeting again were slim to none. Not that he ever wanted to get together with him again. It was fun, he had gotten off, but there was no spark there, no connection. Oscar seemed like a nice guy, but he wasn't someone Clyde could actually see himself spending any real amount of time with.

Then he thought of Evan. They had a good time today working together, getting to know one another. They had so much in common, their choices in movies and games, their political and social beliefs.

And he found Evan so very attractive. He could see himself spending a great deal of time with Evan. He could even imagine a lifetime with him. Not that it would ever happen. Evan seemed smart, witty. He was handsome and an all around nice guy. What the fuck would he want with Clyde?

Besides, he didn't even know if Evan was even gay. And, if he was, would he actually want something with Clyde? Could Clyde actually be that lucky?

Chapter 6

Vices of Men

It was just after midnight when Clyde arrived back home to the trailer. He pulled the old Escort in the drive and parked next to the garage. He pulled the keys from the ignition, climbed out and quietly closed the door.

The living room lights were on in the trailer and he expected to see John alone on the couch when he walked in. Instead, Mamma was sitting in her chair. She was wearing the same dress she had been in all week: brightly colored muumuu with large Hawaiian flowers covering whole sections of the dress. On her feet were faded pink slippers. "What are you doing up, Mamma?" Clyde asked, quietly. John was on the couch, sleeping, his stockinged feet propped up on the coffee table. "Are you feeling alright?"

"Oh, just a little trouble with my breathing. You know how this humidity gets to me," she said, her thick hand waving the air in front of her face as though trying to push more oxygen into her lungs. "Lying down makes it worse. I hoped I could sleep in my chair, but I'm wide awake now. Maybe now that you're home I can go back to bed."

"How are your legs doing?" Clyde asked and squatted down to look at them. Her legs were still bright red, but the bruising on the backs hadn't seemed to spread any. Her legs were dry though and large streaks of flaky white skin ran up the shins. "You want me to put some lotion on them?"

"Oh, could you, deah? They itch wicked bad and you know how hard it is for me to get down there to scratch them."

"You probably shouldn't scratch them anyway. It might get them bleeding." Clyde grabbed the bottle of lotion from the coffee table, pumped a quarter-sized gob in his palm, then rubbed that onto Mamma's left leg. The lotion was greasy and smelled like coconuts, but the white patches immediately disappeared.

"That feels better already," Mamma said.

Clyde glanced over at John. His head was resting on his left shoulder and a soft snore whistled through his nose. A can of beer sat on the coffee table next to his feet. A makeshift coaster of paper towels separated the can from the wooden table. "John's been drinking in the house?" Clyde asked. As long as Clyde could remember, Mamma had a rule about drinking. "Do it if you want, but not in my house." After their father had died, Mamma became somewhat of a teetotaler, rallying against the drink that had killed her husband.

"I changed my mind," Mamma said. "Women can do that now. We got the vote and the pill, now we can even have an opinion." She chuckled softly. "No, I realize we all have vices. Everyone has 'em, 'cause we need 'em. If we didn't have 'em, we'd go crazy. I got my food. I didn't work my way up to five hundred pounds 'cause I like to run, that's for sure." She let out another little laugh, clapped her hand down on her enormous thigh, causing a little breeze of warm air to flutter Clyde's hair. He could smell old sweat in that air. Sweat and something more organic. A smell he sensed was coming from under Mamma's muumuu. "We all need something bad for us, something that wouldn't be bad if we didn't have so much of it."

"And men," she continued, "well, men need more vices than women. They got more worries, more problems. A man needs to take care of his family. Needs to support them. A woman can stay home with the kids, take care of the house. She does that and no one says a thing. But, if a man stays home while the woman works, why, he's no better than a gigolo.

"John's got his drink and his dope. I know you like that dope too, don't you?" Mamma laughed again and ran her thick fingers through Clyde's hair. "It's alright that you smoke that shit. I hear it ain't no more harmful than beer. Probably it ain't, but it's illegal and that's what worries me. I'm so afraid you boys gonna get caught with it. I can't have either one of you in jail. That would kill me, seeing you or John penned up like animals."

Clyde looked up at Mamma and felt the long, heavy drawl of resentment begin to build in him. She hadn't been there for them when their father died. She allowed John to quit school long before he should have to feed her and Clyde. Had forced John to become a man even before he knew what being a man was. Now she was concerned about how much he drank and smoked? He opened his mouth to voice his protests, but stopped himself. Mamma had weaknesses, just like John did. Just like he himself. He couldn't be angry with her for being weak, for being human.

"And John," Mamma continued, "well, he has his women too. Oh, I know he been seeing Darlene for years now, but there been lots others during them years as well. He loves that Darlene though. I can see it on his face. He loves that girl more than he loves himself. That's why he fools around with them others. He don't want to lose himself. That's what happens when a man falls in love, you know. He loses who he is, becomes, I don't know, part of that other person. Happens to women too, but we don't mind it as much. But that's why men need more vices than women. They need them to keep hold of themselves, remind themselves they are men."

Mamma glanced up at the television where a 'reality' show was playing, the volume so low Clyde could barely hear it. The show featured a group of has-been celebrities living in a mansion together and the viewer had the privilege of watching their daily lives. A process which consisted of getting drunk and nearly breaking their necks when they fell down the stairs, or erupting into fist fights with each other. Mamma shook her head, gave the television a disapproving look. "Such foolishness," she said. "Why do these people get paid so much for acting like assholes? I know lots around here that do it for free."

Clyde laughed out loud, then clamped a greasy palm over his mouth before he woke John. He could taste the coconut oil in the lotion and wiped his lips on the back of his hand.

"John said the men he hired started today," Mamma whispered.

"Yeah, they did." Clyde ran his hands up to her knees, then back down to her ankles, spreading the lotion over the worst, driest areas.

"Are they good men? The youngest is your age, right? Evan, is that his name?"

"They seem like good workers. I worked alone with Evan most of the day. He seemed beat by the work, but he kept going. He's a pretty cool guy."

"You like him then?"

"Yeah, I do."

"Good. You need friends, Clyde. You need people your own age. Me and John are family. A man can't survive on just family. You need friends, but you need to start trusting people first."

"I do trust people," Clyde said.

"No you don't. I can tell it in your eyes. You're wary around 'em. Scared almost. I know that look. I see it in my own face every morning when I look in the mirror. Scared, angry. It don't get you nowhere neither."

Clyde pumped more lotion into his palm and began working on the other leg. He felt his cheeks burning and he wouldn't look up at his mother. She was right, he didn't trust people. He was afraid of them because he knew that if he got to know them, they would either leave, like his father, or end up disappointing him, like she did. Or beat the fuck out of him. That's what worried him with John. He knew John loved him, but knew his temper as well, and his hate.

"When your father died," Mamma continued, "I was so mad. I was mad at him for leaving me and mad at God for taking him away. I turned my back on everyone; my friends, family, even you and John. I didn't want to live no more, so I tried to kill myself with one thing that gave me pleasure: food. I thought it would be a beautiful way to die. Eating anything and everything I wanted. I just didn't realize it would take so long.

"Now, I don't want to die, but all this weight has taken it's toll on me. I'm 42 years old and can't walk one end of this trailer to the other without help from this goddamned walker. I can't sleep lying down half the time and haven't seen the outdoors in ye-ahs.

"This is what all that anger and fear has done for me. Don't, Clyde, please don't let it twist you like it did me. Be friends with Evan, don't push him away. I know it's your nature to do that, but you need him. And you know what? He probably needs you, too."

"I'll try, Mamma," Clyde said and he meant it. He would try to trust Evan.

Clyde finished with the lotion, rubbed the film on his hands into his arms and stood. "Thank you, baby," Mamma said.

John stirred on the couch, let out a little snort and turned his head to the right shoulder. "I think I'll go on to bed now. Maybe I can get a few hours sleep. Oh, this humidity is awful." Mamma set her walker in front of the chair and heaved herself upright, her hands gripping the walker so tightly her knuckles turned white. Then, once she was stable, made her way down the hall to her bedroom. The walker clicking like a stopwatch that badly needed winding. Her hips and shoulders brushed both walls of the hallway.

Once, when Clyde was a young boy, there had been pictures on those walls. Framed photographs of Mamma, Dad, John, Clyde, their grandparents and the many, many cousins. It had been a sea of faces. But as Mamma grew wider, the pictures began falling from the walls when she passed by them. To ensure the frames would not be broken, Mamma packed the photos in cardboard boxes and stored them in her bedroom closet. For ten years now the smiling eyes of their family stared into the dark. The memory of what everyone looked like, who everyone was then, were now just memories for Clyde. There was nothing on display to remind him

"It ain't true, what she said about Darlene." Clyde looked over at John, startled by his voice.

"You're awake."

"Yeah, I heard you two old women gossiping 'bout me. I ain't in love with Darlene. Mamma's wrong 'bout that."

"Are you sure?" Clyde asked.

"No. I'm not. Maybe I do love her. All I know is she gives great head," John said, a smile stretching over his face. He patted the couch cushion next to him. "Come sit with me a minute. You want a beer?"

"Sure," Clyde replied and took the can John had pulled from the plastic bag on the floor. It was warm, but felt good going down his throat. It washed the oily coat of semen from his tongue that had grown bitter in his mouth. A rank flavor that reminded Clyde of raw potatoes kept him wishing for a bottle of water or a soda to rinse his mouth all the way home. He had only two dollars in his wallet and didn't want to spend the last of his money on something as frivolous as that, so he drove past all the gas stations and convenience stores on the way home. It felt good to have his mouth washed clean again.

John was wearing an old pair of sweatpants. They had a hole as big as Clyde's palm in the upper thigh, near the crotch. Clyde glanced down at John's bare leg shining out through the hole. At his muscular leg with the sprinkling of coarse, dark hair. He wanted to set his hand on that bare leg. Feel the heat and strength surging through his brother's flesh into his own. He wanted to massage that thigh, feel it lift and move off to the side, giving him access to the heavy basket it walled. Clyde could see John's underwear though the hole. Briefs that had been white when new, now yellowed with age, bleach and piss.

Clyde drained the can and watched as John scratched his leg though the hole in the sweatpants. His fingers running just under the underwear. When he pulled his fingers out a thick tuft of pubic hair stuck out under the leg band, curling around it like a beckoning finger. Seeming to say to Clyde, "What you want is in here. Come and get it." Clyde looked at it and felt the familiar ache growing in him again.

He saw himself moving in between John's legs, pushing his brother's thighs apart while his mouth worked at that hole in his pants, widening it, tearing strips of the material free. In his fantasy he was like a hungry dog, snuffling at John's body, snorting and lapping his way into John's crotch. He could taste the salty tang of the thin layer of sweat coating John's thighs and when he worked his way into the crease of his brother's leg, had the first glimmer of the heat and raw power of what awaited him beneath the underwear.

"Jesus, look at the tits on that one," John said, his eyes glued to the television.

On the television screen the reality show played on. A former porn star, wearing just a tee-shirt and panties, laughed uproariously at the little-person actor — whose most famous role was playing a serial killer troll — who had just fallen off the dining table in a drunken stupor. The porn star's massive breasts bounced like helium-filled balloons as she clamped her fists to her sides to calm herself.

"Oh man, I'd like to give that one a good titty fucking," John said and squeezed his crotch through the sweatpants. The underwear lifted slightly as he did this and the wrinkled flesh of his scrotum peeked out through the worn leg hole. Clyde could feel the snuffling dog in him begging to get back to work again. Could hear it whimper as Clyde held it back by it's collar. "Bad dog," he silently ordered it.

Clyde downed the rest of the beer and clapped John on the leg. His hand smacking the bare flesh through the hole in the sweatpants. He could feel the rough hair against his palm, sense the heat coming off his brother and Clyde felt the surge of his own blood rushing into his nether regions. "I'm going to bed," he said and rose from the couch, keeping his back to John to hide his growing erection.

"Me, too," John said. "We have to be up in four hours." John turned off the television and followed Clyde down the hall. "Good night, bro," John said as Clyde entered his bedroom while John continued down the hall to his own.

Clyde stripped to his boxers and slid into bed. He thought about Oscar and the taste of his cock. Thought about how it felt when Oscar pushed himself down Clyde's throat, going deeper than he had allowed any man to get. It hurt and scared him a little, having his air choked off like that. But he liked it as well. It had tested his boundaries, like a runner testing his limits in a marathon.

He slid his hands into his boxers, felt himself growing hard at the memory. He ran his thumb over the head of his dick and caught a drop of pre-come, pulled it up to his face and let it string between his thumb and index finger a few times, then slid his fingers into his mouth. He liked the taste of it, much more than the fluid that came after. This was light and sweet, almost like corn syrup. He pulled on his cock, working the liquid flowing out the urethra to coat his palm, then slowly slid his hand up and down, working himself closer to orgasm.

He thought about Oscar wanting him to say the N-word and his erection dwindled. John would have said it. If a black man wanted John to say the word, he would probably do it. John never said it because even he knew it was one of the most socially unacceptable, most vile of words. Of course, John would say it if asked, but he would not have been in the position Clyde had been. He would not be on his knees with a black man's cock down his throat, or any man's for that matter. Clyde imagined the look on John's face if he happened to see Clyde down there, on his knees, sucking off Oscar in that picnic area. He imagined John would go batshit seeing Clyde go down on any man, but a black man? Jesus, it would be like the end of the world. He would probably do more than knock one of Clyde's teeth out. He would probably kill him, beat him to death.

Yes, John was controlled by his fear, but then Clyde realized he was, too. He avoided people in town because he was afraid: if they found out about him, about his unorthodox sex life, he would be shunned. It was better to shun them first.

But he knew John wouldn't find out. It was best if he didn't because there are some things that just have to stay secret.

He thought about John and that hole in his pants, the leg beneath it and the old underwear holding him in. His erection sprang back to life. He had fantasized about John so long, for so many years, it was almost second nature to him. The moment his hand wrapped around his dick, images of John's body, hot and sweaty, naked with his arms spread wide, waiting to take Clyde into his loving embrace, filled his head.

He imagined now, his face buried in John's hairy chest, smelling the pine and sawdust on him. He imagined John's cock pressing against him, grinding into his own dick as John lay on top of him. John's mouth moving in for a kiss, which Clyde would gladly give him, but the moment their lips touched, John was gone. In his place was another man. The lips were just as delectable though, just as soft and tender. The body just as beautiful as well. He looked into the new man's eyes. They were a pale hazel, like John's, but one was looking at him, the other to the left. "Evan," Clyde whispered.

That was when he came.

Chapter 7

The Invitation

All morning Clyde felt as though he were walking through some weird, translucent goo. Encased in a strange jelly-like substance that was there, in his bedroom when his alarm clock pulled him from what turned out to be a two hour nap at four o'clock and followed him out to the kitchen where he downed his first coffee of the day with a bowl of corn flakes. A second coffee followed after a quick shower, but before brushing his teeth. A third went into his travel mug and journeyed with him to the work site off Pine Hill Road.

"You look like shit," John said as he checked the gas and oil levels in his chainsaw. It had been a mostly quiet ride, except the yammering of the right-wing nut on the talk radio station John nearly always kept the radio tuned to, and Clyde actually felt himself drift off to sleep at one point. His face pressed against the door glass like a lonely puppy in a pet shop window.

"Thanks," Clyde replied. He and Evan had completed their saw checks the previous afternoon in preparation of this morning, so Clyde sat on the tailgate and watched his brother work.

"That's what you get for wasting your night getting high with a douchebag like Fred."

The excess of caffeine couldn't seem to shake the odd out-of-body feel the lack of sleep had on him. Everything seemed to be moving in slow motion, like a scene in a movie where the film is slowed down to capture every nuance of a particular action sequence. It seemed like minutes passed from when Clyde thought about lifting his arm and his hand actually appeared before his face. It was a little frightening, with his mind moving this slow and knowing he had to run a chainsaw most of the day.

When Dale's truck pulled into the lot and Evan climbed out of the passenger side, a travel mug of his own firmly gripped in his hand, Clyde's mind seemed to snap to attention. His penis sat up and took notice as well. He now felt more alert and rested than if he had twelve hours sleep instead of just two.

He watched Evan grab his gear from the back of Dale's truck. Hard hat, ear protection and chainsaw — fluid levels already checked — then juggle them along with his coffee cup over to where Clyde and John stood. "Morning," Evan said, his right eye looking directly into Clyde's left. A long, slow smile spread over his face. He quickly glanced over at John. "Good morning John," he said with almost casual disinterest, then turned his attention back to Clyde. The smile grew wider and Clyde felt himself return the smile.

"You guys ready to cut some wood?" John asked, then threw on his own helmet, pulled the screen visor down over his face and marched up the narrow trail to the spot they would be working. Dale raced ahead to walk beside John while Clyde and Evan lagged behind.

"Are you okay, Clyde? Your eyes are wicked red. You aren't high already, are you?" Evan asked as they walked along the hard, crusted path.

"No, I..." Clyde started. He was about to give Evan the same lie he had handed to John, but he couldn't do it. He couldn't lie to Evan. That was strange because he had no problem spilling the lie to his older brother John, a man who had raised him from the age of five, who had sacrificed his own education and future so Clyde could possibly have a better life than he did. He couldn't lie to Evan, but couldn't tell him the truth either. So he simply gave the excuse, "I couldn't sleep."

"Oh, this is going to be a rough day then."

"Nah, I can handle it. I've done it before."

"I was going to ask you... um, if you wanted to... uh, hang out or something after work. If you want to do that, but are too tired tonight, we can do it some other time," Evan said. He took large swallows during each pause as though he were nervous. As though something very important weighed in Clyde's reply.

"What did you have in mind?" Clyde asked, feeling his pulse suddenly slam through his veins, his heart speeding so fast he grew dizzy. He could almost see himself fainting into Evan's arms, like some southern belle in an old black and white melodrama. *He likes me!* he thought. *Enough to want to hang out with me. Maybe not the way I like him, but it's something.*

"I just picked up the new *Battlelines* game last night, *Wars of Our Fathers*. I haven't had a chance to check it out yet, but I thought I'd order a pizza and we could try the game together. But... I mean, if you didn't get much sleep last night, we can always do it another time."

"No, it'll be fun," Clyde quickly replied, doing his best to keep too much excitement from pouring out of him. He didn't want to seem desperate to spend some alone time with Evan, even though he really was.

Evan stopped walking, the chainsaw dangling from his hand, blade pointed at the ground. "It's okay Clyde, we can do it another time."

"Evan, tell me where you live because I'm coming over tonight. I'll sleep when I'm dead. Besides, days like this are what caffeine is for."

"Cool." Evan gave Clyde directions. He lived on Pleasant Lake Road. Clyde knew the area: it was on the west side of town and the road was paved for the first two miles, then turned to dirt. Evan lived a mile onto the rough, dusty, unpaved section. In the four miles of dirt road, there were only about six homes. It was isolated and rural compared to the trailer park Clyde lived in.

With the excitement of his impending evening with Evan shining ahead, time slowed to a tongue dragging crawl for Clyde. When lunch finally arrived, after what seemed an eon had passed, Clyde and Evan sat together on one of the trees they had brought down, gobbling their sandwiches and guzzling from gallon jugs of water. "No soda today, huh?" Clyde said as Evan tipped back the water jug, the liquid spilling out the corners of his mouth, saturating his shirt.

Clyde watched the water cascade over Evan. Stared as it soaked the thick fistful of hair sticking out of the top of the teeshirt and he saw himself licking Evan dry. Even with the sweat and muck covering him, Clyde still wanted to pull that water from Evan with his tongue.

"No. I think I was getting dehydrated yesterday. I felt kind of light headed, sort of like I was high, but not in a fun way. Like when you're stoned at a family get-together or something and have to act sober."

"Do you do that often, puffing before a family party?"

"I try not to. Do you know what it's like trying to carry on a conversation with your grandmother while you're stoned off your ass? It's not fun, I can guarantee you that."

When six o'clock finally came, the four men left in two directions: Dale to drop Evan off at his car in the credit union parking lot, John and Clyde for home. John stopped at Miller's on the way home to get a single beer, using the last two dollars in his wallet. Clyde grabbed a two liter of soda, using the last of his money. It was only Tuesday and they were both now officially broke.

"So, what were you two girls giggling about all day?" John asked once they were back in the truck.

"We weren't giggling," Clyde said, though he did feel a giggle coming on in anticipation and expectation of the coming evening with Evan.

"Tee-heeing then."

"Evan invited me over to play video games," Clyde said, forcing his voice to sound as nonchalant as possible.

"Ooh, you guys are really hitting it off. Should I be jealous?" John laughed and clapped his palm onto Clyde's leg. Clyde felt the sting, even through the insulated coveralls.

When they arrived home, Clyde quickly kissed Mamma hello, then ran to the bathroom to shower. Standing in his room wearing just a towel, he grabbed a clean pair of jeans from the closet and dug through the small dresser built into the wall for a shirt that wasn't threadbare or had holes. He found just two that fit the requirement. One was tight around his chest, which had grown much harder and more muscular in the last year working with John in the woods every day, the other featured a group of cartoon characters dressed like 1940's G-Men. He stood debating for a moment, should he go with tight and sexy, or goofy and fun? He decided on sexy.

He thought about sneaking into John's room and using some of his cologne, then thought against it. He didn't want to seem like he was actually trying to impress Evan. Evan had, after all, invited him to play video games, not a candle lit dinner and dancing. Yet, he hoped tonight would be the start of something between them. If not something sexual or — *gulp!* — romantic, then at least another step in their friendship. Mamma was right, he needed friends his own age. He couldn't be happy with just family.

He stepped into the living room, keys in hand. Mamma gave him a wolf whistle. "Don't you look nice. Is that a new shirt?" she asked.

"No, I just haven't worn it in a while."

"Well, it really shows off your arms. You got some muscle on you now. How did that happen?"

John stepped in from the kitchen. He leaned against the wall, arms crossed over his chest. "All set for your big date, huh?"

Clyde felt the heat rushing into his face. He could feel embarrassment creeping up on him, ready to lay him out with his own shame. He had nothing to be ashamed of, though. They were just two guys getting together to play video games. If something happened — *please, please, please let something happen* — he would let it happen. But he wasn't going to anticipate or expect anything. And if they did happen to fool around, John never had to know about it. "Fuck you, John," he said, letting the guise of anger cover his embarrassment.

John pushed himself from the wall and stepped up to Clyde. Their faces just inches apart. John's face hard and stern, Clyde forced his features to match his brothers. He was scared, but the anger he had just feigned, was becoming real. John was trying to intimidate him, just as he had their entire lives and it occurred to Clyde then, he didn't have to allow John to threaten him any longer. He had as much right to live his life his way, just as anyone else.

Clyde's hands were at his sides and he felt them moving. He looked down and saw the fingers curling in on the palms, then opening. He was involuntarily flexing and relaxing his fists, just as John did before throwing himself into a fight. He took several deep breaths, calmed himself and prepared himself to feel John's fist striking his face. Instead John laughed, reached around Clyde and gave him a playful pat on the bottom. "Remember, if he tries to touch you, tell him you are not that kind of girl. Nothing until you get a ring," he said, then stepped out of Clyde's way.

"I'll be home later, Mamma," Clyde said, bent over the recliner and kissed her cheek.

"Have fun, De-ah," Mamma said as Clyde walked out the door and gently closed it behind him. He jogged out to his Escort, started it, then noticed his gas gauge hovering just above the quarter tank mark. It was only about eight miles to Pleasant Lake and back. He knew he had plenty of gas. *The only thing that matters though,* he thought, *is getting there.*

Chapter 8
With Evan

Clyde was startled when the pavement of Pleasant Lake Road abruptly ended and the dirt and gravel section began. It seemed to come out of nowhere, like he was driving off a cliff. Clyde had only been out in this neighborhood a few times — if a small collection of six abodes in a four mile stretch could be considered a neighborhood — and when the rough, narrow dirt road loomed ahead of him he instinctively slammed on the brakes. The road narrowed from a mostly smooth two lane stretch of blacktop, rough and cracked, but still paved, to a single lane potholed dirt path.

Clyde slowed his Escort down to crawling speed, the needle hovering around the 15 MPH mark as he wove all the way to the left side of the road, then back to the right to avoid the most ominous looking potholes. He still managed to hit the majority of the smaller ones. The car rattled and banged against each small drop and he began to sweat the suspension system. He wasn't sure what condition it was in, but after traveling up this road he might need to have it looked at.

The houses along Pleasant Lake were mostly old farmhouses. Evan's home was the only new one. It was a double-wide trailer on a single lot set here in just the last year.

Clyde saw it as he rounded a very sharp and very terrifying corner. If another vehicle had of been coming the other way neither Clyde or the other driver would have seen one another and they might have collided. But there was no other vehicle and as he made the hairpin turn, he saw in the distance on a flat stretch, the double-wide.

His pulse immediately began to quicken and sweat beaded on his forehead. *This isn't a date*, he told himself, but it sure as shit felt like one. He was sweating like a virgin on her honeymoon. His palms were slick, sweat trickled down his back, collecting in his underwear and his heart was beating like he had run a mile.

He pulled in the driveway and sat for a few seconds trying to calm himself. The lot around the trailer had been cleared. The shrubs, trees and wild scrub had been pushed back at least thirty feet from all sides of Evan's home. The lawn — which was not really a lawn yet — was covered in hay to protect the grass seed sewn into the soil from hungry birds and squirrels. When the grass eventually made an appearance, Clyde could see this would be a beautiful piece of land.

He pulled the key from the ignition, exited the car while wiping his nervous palms on his jeans and, with slightly shaky legs, climbed the few steps up to the front door and raised his hand to knock. The door opened before his knuckles could connect. Evan stood on the other side of the screened storm door, that gorgeous smile pouring from his handsome face.

"You made it," Evan said with a voice that sounded as excited and nervous as Clyde felt.

"You give great directions," Clyde said, holding up the 2-liter bottle of Coke he bought at Miller's on the way home from work. "I remembered you brought Coke to work yesterday, seemed like a safe bet."

"You didn't have to bring anything. But since you did, let's get it in the refrigerator." Evan opened the screen door, inviting Clyde inside. Evan was shower fresh, his curly black hair still wet and lying over his head in moist rings. When Clyde stepped inside could smell the strawberry shampoo in Evan's hair. He smelled good and Clyde wanted to press his face into the thick mop, inhale him like a drug.

Evan had changed into a baggy tee-shirt and loose shorts. His thin, furry legs bare from just six inches below his hips down to the short crew socks at mid-shin. Instantly Clyde's body responded and he held the bottle in front of his crotch to hide the evidence.

Evan took the bottle from him, glancing down as he did. A smile quickly flickered over his face before he turned to set the soda in the refrigerator. A large pizza box took up the majority of the small kitchen table. *Donovan's*, the box exclaimed in bright red letters, *The best pizza east of Chicago.* Clyde had a Donovan's pizza once, long ago and honestly couldn't remember if it was good enough to proclaim it was the best east of Chicago, and didn't really care. He wasn't here for the pizza. He could feel the heat coming from the box as he turned away to glance around the room.

Clyde was surprised at the kitchen. It was small, but clean. The walls were papered with tiny blue cornflowers against a shimmering white background and even with night coming and only two small windows in the walls and a skylight in the ceiling, the room had a bright and sunny feel to it.

The living room was equally impressive. The ceiling stretched up 12 feet to a cathedral ceiling. A fan slowly pulling the warm air up to the mock rafters. A gas fireplace held the prominent position in the room though. A mantle over the fireplace held framed photographs of Dale and his wife, a black and white still of a handsome, middle-aged couple that Clyde assumed was Evan's parents and a shot of a German Shepard, its tongue lolling out of its happy mouth. Evan looked just like his mother. He had the same dark, curly hair and twinkling smile she did in the photo.

"This place is gorgeous," Clyde said, thinking of his own trailer, a 1982 model that hadn't had a proper cleaning since before he could read.

"Thanks. I bought it last year. Had it moved in here to be closer to Dale."

"Where are you from originally?" Clyde asked, feeling a little self-conscious asking, like he was prying.

"Vermont. Our parents still live out there. Dale's wife is from here though."

"Cool."

They looked at each other a moment. Clyde was unsure if he should direct the conversation from here or even what he should say. Finally Evan broke the silence. "I was hit by a car when I was a kid. That's how I got this," he said and pointed at his lazy eye. "Head trauma. The doctors said it might come back to normal eventually, but it never did. Anyway, that's how I bought this place. I got a settlement that went into a trust fund until I turned eighteen."

"I like it," Clyde blurted out before he had a chance to reconsider what he was saying.

"You like what? My fucked up eye?"

"Yeah... I mean, yeah, I do. It gives you character."

"Most people think I'm simple because of it. You know, like I'm mentally retarded or something."

"Those people are morons," Clyde said. He wanted to tell Evan what he really thought. He wanted to tell Evan how intelligent, witty, and clever he was. How Evan was unlike nearly everyone Clyde had known in his eighteen years. And how special Evan made him feel just by associating with him. But, he didn't say any of that. Instead he stood with his hands in his back pockets and struggled not to undress Evan with his eyes.

Evan pulled a couple of paper plates from the cupboard, handed one to Clyde, then opened the pizza box. Heat radiated from the food in humid streams. Evan had apparently just returned from Donovan's Pizza before Clyde had arrived. "Dig in," he said. "We can eat while we play." He tore a dozen paper towels from the holder hanging near the sink, handed them to Clyde, then tore another dozen free for himself.

Clyde dropped a single slice of the pepperoni pizza on his plate. The crust was golden brown, and when he lifted the slice from the rest, the bubbly mozzarella cheese clung to the rest in long stringy strips. The combined smells of cheese, tomato and greasy pepperoni made Clyde's belly growl in anticipation of the food. He hadn't realized how hungry he was until now; the sandwich he had at lunch had long since been digested. He stood back to let Evan fill his own plate. "Take two," Evan said, pulled a slice from the box and dropped it on Clyde's plate, then grabbed a few for himself. They took their food into the living room, sat on the couch, then Evan dashed back to the kitchen to grab the bottle of Coke Clyde had brought, along with a set of plastic cups.

Evan grabbed the television remote control, hit the power button, then fired up the gaming console. They both ate while the welcoming screen started on the game. *Battlelines: Wars of Our Fathers* exploded in bright splashes across the screen, in gray letters like the iron body of a battleship, complete with rivets and in hot red slashes resembling flesh wounds. Evan handed Clyde a game controller. Clyde took it after thoroughly wiping his hands on the paper towels. Clyde had played one of the *Battlelines* games before at Fred's and was familiar with the controls and the general object of the game. It was a first person shooter and the goal, like most games like this, was to kill everything in sight.

They played, taking bites of their pizza, washing it down with Coke and rubbing their fingers incessantly on the paper towels to clear them of the orange pizza grease. All the while, Clyde sneaked glances at Evan. Evan had a bright smile and the intense squint at the television as he fired and fired and ran his character through obstacles and danger zones revealed how much he enjoyed playing the game. Nearly as much, Clyde thought, as he enjoyed watching Evan. He snuck looks at those gorgeous legs, pale, hairy, faintly muscle toned, adorable knobby knees bent. He wanted to run his hands up those legs. He wanted to feel them as they spread for him, press his face between the furry thighs, feel the bulge in Evan's shorts expand with his touch.

As they played and Clyde's peeks became more and more common, his eyes would catch Evan's face turned to him, looking at him in the same way. Quick glances at Clyde's firm chest in the too tight shirt, rapid peeks at his muscled biceps, the thick blue veins in his forearms as his hands flexed with the manipulation of the game controller. They were studying each other, Clyde realized. Watching each other with the intensity of two predators in the wild, but each hiding their examinations with the guise of human civility. He glanced at Evan with thoughts of lust weighing on his mind. But, he wondered, how was Evan looking at him? Was it the same? Was it sexual curiosity that drew his attention or was he simply watching Clyde, a new friend, for signs of his deeper emotional makeup? To see if Clyde really was worth his friendship.

Their eyes met and each quickly turned away, a nervous laugh erupting from both of them. It happened once, twice, then on the third encounter they did not turn away. They kept their eyes locked to one another, held their stares. Evan grinned, a quiver of nervousness on his smiling face. Clyde stared at those lips, shiny with pizza grease, those beautiful lips he wanted to touch with his own. Lips he wanted to taste.

So he did. He leaned in and pressed his mouth to Evan's mouth, gently yet firmly enough to taste the pepperoni, gooey cheese and Coca-Cola on his lips. He felt each wrinkle, each line in Evan's lips on his own, felt the ridge of his thin, red mouth. The connection was heavenly. The most beautiful moment of his life so far. Kissing a man he not only found so stunningly attractive, but also a monumentally extraordinary person. A beautiful man in and out.

That is, until Evan snapped away from Clyde's touch, a look of shock on his face. Shock and yes, was that disgust he saw there in Evan's eyes? Disgust and repulsion at Clyde's mouth on his. And was there anger in the mix? Yes, it was there. He knew he saw a near uncontrollable rage flash over Evan's face.

How dare Clyde think Evan would want him? How much gall did Clyde have to think that Evan, bright, handsome, wonderful Evan would ever want someone as lowly and fucked-in-the-head as Clyde?

Panic erupted in him with volcanic pressure, tearing him from the couch, pushing him to the door. "I'm sorry... I... I'm sorry," he stammered, his head spinning in terror.

You fucking idiot, his mind screamed. *You screwed this up, you screwed yourself with your fucked up abnormal lusts. You don't deserve Evan, or anyone for that matter, as a lover or a friend. You deserve to be alone. Fucking idiot!*

"I misread... oh, I'm sorry."

"Clyde," he heard from behind him, but he ignored the voice. Ignored the gentle understanding in the voice.

Clyde reached the front door, grabbed the handle and turned it. It spun uselessly in his fist. His hands were slick with pizza grease. He wiped them on his pants and tried again. His hand still slicked around the handle, frictionless, spinning around the metal knob.

He felt the tears coming then. His eyes filling with exhausted self-depreciation. He had slept only two hours in the last thirty-six and his tired mind and body struggled to hold them in, yet a few escaped and trickled down his cheeks.

"Clyde," the voice behind him again. Hands, on his back, gentle, caressing hands. They touched his shoulders and turned him. He allowed himself to be turned, but kept his head low. He wouldn't look at Evan, wouldn't let Evan see him cry. He would not show weakness.

He would not allow Evan to see him crying like a boy who lost his favorite toy... or a man who has destroyed his first chance at happiness.

Mamma is right: I push people away. I am alone because I secretly know I deserve to be alone. If I can't push potential friends away by normal means, I throw myself at them, ensuring they will leave me in disgust. I am repulsive.

"Clyde, look at me," Evan said. But Clyde wouldn't, even when Evan took his chin between his thumb and forefinger and lifted his head. He kept his eyes focused on the floor. Stared through the rippling tears at the tiles. If he looked up and saw the hate he knew must be there in Evan's face, he would shatter like a pane of glass. He would be destroyed and like Humpty Dumpty, would never be put back together again. He would be lost forever.

"Clyde, look at me. Please." He heard something in that voice. A shaky quivering, a sad pleading. It hurt him to hear it. Hurt that maybe he had not enraged Evan, but struck him on some other level. Had perhaps, caused Evan to hurt as Clyde now did.

He took the chance and turned his eyes up to meet Evan's. He was ready to feel his brain explode, ready to see the disappointment on Evan's face, effectively ending their very short-lived friendship. He saw instead, wet, red rimmed eyes looking back at him. "I'm sorry I pulled back like that. You just surprised me, that's all," Evan said, still holding Clyde's chin in his fingers. "I've wanted to kiss you all day. You beat me to it."

Clyde let himself go then, let the tears flow. But, there was no need for them now. Evan wanted him. Could this actually be possible? Could this be real? Then he felt Evan's mouth on his, felt his own mouth open and Evan's tongue slide inside. Felt his tongue touched by Evan's tongue. He tilted his head, their lips hungrily worked against, then with each other. The kiss went on for minutes, hours, days. A lifetime of unrequited crushes and secret longing smashed against the draw of this beautiful mouth.

Chapter 9
Building the Bridge

The kiss carried Clyde and Evan, still connected, back to the couch. The pizza, soda and war game forgotten. They had something better to eat and play with. Clyde hooked his fingers in the base of Evan's shirt, pulled it up, exposing his furry torso, and broke the kiss just long enough to clear the material past their faces. He tossed the shirt behind him, hearing it flutter to the thick carpet somewhere on the living room floor, then dove back into that warm, inviting mouth. He ran his hands along Evan's body, feeling the thick mat of hair on his belly and chest brush his palm. He had to see it. He had to see what his hands saw, had to see the body that he knew needed to be explored further with his eyes and hands and mouth.

He felt Evan tugging on his own shirt. He sat upright, lifted his arms so he could be freed of his clothes and heard a groan of appreciation from Evan. He felt Evan's mouth on his chest, teeth at his nipples and a wet tongue lapping at his armpit. "You are so fucking gorgeous," Evan said and Clyde was pulled down on top of him. Hands clamped around Clyde's back, ankles crossed over his buttocks as he was firmly secured to this beautiful man. Their cocks, separated by Clyde's jeans and Evan's shorts pressed against one another, attempted not only to excite one another, but to meld into one fat organ. Each man sharing pleasure and quivering, physical excitement.

Clyde reached down between them, tugged on the cotton shorts clinging to Evan's hips. He lifted himself from Evan to free the garment. He pushed them down over those beautiful legs, pausing only to caress the thighs, to feel his fingers dance through the thick, dark carpet covering those legs and tossed the shorts as carelessly as he had the shirt. Evan wore white briefs underwear, the same type John wore. These came off even more quickly than the shorts. The hard ridge of Evan's cock, hot and pulsating, sprang loose once the confining underwear met the floor. Clyde stared at it a moment. Long and fat with a dark circumcision scar ringing the bright red, nearly purple head. His balls dangled low in the heat of the day, covered in curls of dark hair. Clyde immediately dipped his face into them. The raw, musky man stink filled his sinuses. His head swam, drunk with want. He let each big, sweat-coated ball bounce over his tongue and he lapped down below them into the recesses of the furry ass crack.

A sweet moan escaped Evan's lips. A shuddering groan. Fingers forcefully tugged at Clyde's hair, pulling him up to the fat cock head. A steady stream of clear, wet pearls dribbled from the tip. Clyde lapped at them, the sweet nectar coating his tongue. The cock tensed with each touch of his tongue. Bounced against Evan's furry belly, then back against Clyde's lips as though wanting to dive between them. Clyde opened his mouth and pulled it in, savoring the control he had over Evan. He pushed himself down, swallowing the fat pole until his lips met the course, wiry patch of hair at Evan's groin, then pulled back up again, suckling at inch after inch as it left his mouth. He savored the pleasured groans, reveled in the quivering ticks rippling through Evan's body as he drew him closer to orgasm. He wanted to feel him erupt in his mouth. Wanted to taste his seed as it coated the back of his throat.

But Evan wasn't ready for that now. He pushed Clyde off his cock. Clyde fought him, refusing to give up his prize. "Clyde, stop. I'm too close. I don't want to come yet," Evan said. Reluctantly, Clyde did as requested.

Evan stood. "Sit down on the sofa."

Clyde complied without protest. Evan dropped between Clyde's feet and pulled off his boots. The tan, Herman Survivor steel toe work boots—the only shoes Clyde owned—slid off his feet and Evan gently set them on the floor beside the couch. He handled them like they were fragile, like they were valuable idols to worship. He pulled Clyde's socks off him, then slid up the length of Clyde's body, dropping wet, sucking kisses along his belly and chest. He lapped at Clyde's nipples again, teasing them with his teeth until shivers ran up Clyde's back and goose flesh rose along his neck and arms.

"You like that?" Evan asked. Clyde nodded his head that he did. He didn't dare speak. Tears were dangerously close to filling his eyes and spilling down his cheeks again. Not because he was afraid or hurt this time. It was because he had never allowed anyone to touch him like this before. It was too dangerous. If he enjoyed being with someone like this he might start to have feelings for them beyond the sex. If he had feelings for someone, then his world would change, forever.

Clyde realized then, it didn't really matter what he and Evan did together. He already had feelings for him. Evan's hands and mouth on him only intensified those feelings.

Evan leaned back and said, "Stand up." He paused a moment, then followed with, "Please."

Clyde did as asked and Evan fumbled with the buckle on Clyde's jeans, then pulled them, along with his boxers, down to the floor. Clyde stepped out of his clothes and stood, naked and vulnerable, before Evan.

"Oh wow," Evan groaned, on his knees before Clyde. He looked up at him, seemingly soaking in every inch of Clyde's body. He ran his fingers up Clyde's legs. Past the thick, uncircumcised cock that stood up from his groin, stretched past his belly button and reached for the hard, rippled muscles of his belly, to Clyde's firm chest. Evan stared at the cock before him, the rubbery foreskin pulled back enough to give a glimpse of the moist head beneath. "It's big," Evan said with an echo of wonder in his voice, a fascinated, greedy joy.

Clyde took his words as something else though. He heard exasperation in the voice. Fear, that he couldn't accomplish what he felt Clyde wanted him to do. "You don't have to, if you don't want," Clyde said. After the random encounters in the picnic area, when he serviced men and didn't expect reciprocation because he might not get it, or deserve it, he could only expect the same from Evan. After all, Evan was stunningly handsome, in Clyde's opinion. How could he expect someone so attractive to sully himself, to dirty himself by sucking on Clyde's unworthy cock?

"Like hell I don't," Evan said and enthusiastically pulled Clyde into his mouth.

It was like a thousand mouths touching him everywhere at once.

The soft lips, pulling him into the warm, wet mouth immediately softened the muscles in his legs and buttocks and he had all he could do to stay upright. Every nerve ending in his body seemed to erupt in vibrant, tingling sensations that ran up and down his spine and soared through each limb. The current reached the tips of his fingers and toes, then spun around and moved back to his shoulders and hips, only to do the same thing there and head back down his arms and legs again.

He could feel every ridge and bump of Evan's tongue as it squirmed over his cock. As it wormed in under the foreskin, then lie flat as Evan pulled in every inch of Clyde's rather oversized cock, until his lips meshed with Clyde's thatch of dark pubic hair.

Clyde could feel the back of Evan's mouth, then the tight throat muscles milking his cock head as he was pulled down into Evan's gullet. The warm, wet bath Evan was giving him was nearly too much. He could feel the orgasm building already.

Clyde nearly made him stop when Evan emitted a loud retch like he was about to vomit. He didn't want to hurt Evan and whatever pleasure Clyde was feeling, and there was a great deal of pleasure, was not worth making Evan uncomfortable. But then Clyde looked down and saw the joy on Evan's upturned face. The wide smile as their eyes met and Evan seductively lapped at the wet, glistening head, then plunged himself back down on his cock. He enjoyed giving Clyde this pleasure as much as Clyde enjoyed receiving it.

He was so close now, so damned close to coming he tried to think of something that would bring him back down again. Something that would hold off the inevitable for just a few more minutes. Nothing surfaced. "I'm going to come in your mouth, Evan. You better pull off me."

When he looked down, Evan didn't retreat as he expected him to. Instead he worked more furiously on him. The smile wrapped around Clyde's girth was even more exuberant. Evan seemed to want to taste Clyde. He seemed to want his mouth to be filled with Clyde's seed. Evan wanted him.

That thought sent him over the edge. Evan wanted him!

The orgasm tore through Clyde like a firestorm. He felt everything in him ignite. Stars exploded in his head and he grabbed Evan by the shoulders to steady himself before he was pitched head first over him. His cock erupted and he felt Evan swallow and swallow as his mouth filled to overflowing.

Shudders rippled through Clyde's body as he collapsed backwards onto the couch. His cock slid from Evan's mouth with a slick *plop*. He panted, struggled to breathe as his heart slammed in his chest. He had had intense orgasms before, but never like this. Evan pulled trickles of sticky, semen from his chin with his forefinger, then slid the finger into his mouth with a satisfied sigh. "Yummy," he said.

The power of the orgasm as well as the realization that Evan wanted to touch him like this brought tears to Clyde's eyes.

"Jesus, I didn't think I was that good," Evan said as he wiped the tears running down Clyde's cheeks with his thumb.

"You're amazing," Clyde said. He scooted to the edge of the couch cushion as Evan rose to his feet. Evan's erection pointed at the ceiling. His balls had grown tight in the scrotum, like a small fist. Pre-come oozed from the head in a thick, syrupy river. Clyde lapped Evan dry, then pulled him into his mouth. He was back on familiar territory now, the giver of pleasure.

Evan could last no longer than Clyde had. After just a few moments of sucking on him, of pulling his sweet cock down into his throat, Clyde tasted the eruption of the sweet, bitter fluid. Evan grabbed Clyde's head, held him as he thrust himself further down Clyde's throat. He let out a strangled cry as his body quivered and shook. Clyde couldn't breathe, but he didn't care at that point. Evan tasted too good to worry about a minor thing such as breathing.

Finally Evan released Clyde and fell onto the couch next to him. Clyde leaned into Evan, pushed him until he was lying on the couch, then curled himself next to him. He kissed Evan's mouth, cheeks and throat. "What were the tears for?" Evan asked, his voice so low Clyde could barely hear him though he was only inches away.

"I don't know," Clyde lied. He knew perfectly well why he had cried after the orgasm. By allowing Evan to touch him like that, he was starting to reconnect with humanity. As though he was building a bridge with his own hands and heart. Setting the structural supports in place, planing the boards and hammering them in place. He only had to cross over to where the rest of the world waited for him.

He was forcing a change in himself because if he didn't, this life of loneliness would be the only thing he would ever know. Clyde could not live like that anymore, but building this bridge meant change. Change, whether it leads to a better life or not, is almost always painful. "I guess you make me feel..." he paused a moment to consider what he was about to say. "You make me feel worthy."

"Worthy?"

"Yeah, like I have a right to feel as good as what you made me feel."

"You do have the right."

"Do I?" Clyde asked, not really sure he believed it.

"Yeah. You know what? You're going to feel that good again," Evan replied as he reached down between them, took Clyde's cock in his hand and slowly stroked him until his cock stood at its full height. He slid down the couch until he was between Clyde's legs. He opened his mouth and quickly pulled Clyde into him.

This time, thoughts of whether he deserved this or not never entered Clyde's head. He simply lay back and enjoyed it.

Chapter 10
Momma Goes Out

The trailer shook with a such a quick, booming quake, Clyde was nearly pitched from his bed. He jumped to his feet, his foggy mind still held firmly in sleep, wondering if the trailer's shudder had actually happened or was part of an elaborate dream. "Terrorists! The fucking Muslims are attacking!" he heard John yell from his bedroom and knew that the trailer had indeed been shaken. He ran out into the hall, nearly collided with John in the process. John, like Clyde, was in his underwear. He had an erection that tented the elastic band of his briefs so far from his belly that when Clyde glanced down, he could see the root of John's cock, nestled in the dark thatch of wiry hair. John's eyes were puffy with sleep and his hair stuck out of his scalp in nearly every direction, giving him the appearance, Clyde thought, of one of those Japanese Anime characters. He nearly let out a giggle until he remembered what had woken them.

"Mamma," they said in unison. They ran out to the living room and there she was, sprawled on the floor, the coffee table lying in pieces under her. She had fallen on it and all four of its legs had broken under her immense weight. The table was split down the middle. The television remote control, Mamma's bottle of lotion and all the other assorted junk that usually littered the table were strewn around the room. Mamma lay with her back against the couch, clutching her left shoulder. Her lips were purple.

"Oh... oh," she moaned.

John pushed past Clyde and dropped to the floor beside her. He took her hand in his. "Mamma, what happened?" he asked. Clyde suspected, with the purple lips, that it was her heart. He ran to the

70

phone and dialed 9-1-1.

"It hurts," Mamma groaned, her right hand clutched madly. The flower print muumuu bunched in her fist, pulling up to reveal her red and bruised legs up to the knees.

"9-1-1, how may I assist you?" a pleasant, almost cheerful voice came through the cordless handpiece pressed to Clyde's ear.

"We think Mamma is having a heart attack. We need an ambulance," Clyde quickly blurted. He gave the operator their name and address. "Please, please send help now."

The 9-1-1 operator confirmed the address, then said, "The ambulance is on its way, sir. Do you have any aspirin? Give her some aspirin right now. It may prevent damage to the heart."

"John," Clyde said. "She wants us to give her some aspirin. I think there is some in the bathroom."

"Aspirin?" John screamed. "She ain't got a fucking headache, she's having a hah-t attack for Christ's sake!" But John jumped to his feet anyway, ran to the bathroom and returned a few seconds later with the bottle in his fist. He dumped a half dozen of the little white pills into his palm and dropped them into Mamma's mouth. "Chew these up," he said.

Mamma did as instructed. "Oh, they're bitt-ah," she complained. "Get me some soda to wash them down. They're horrible."

Clyde went to the refrigerator, the phone still at his ear. There was half a bottle of flat orange soda on the top shelf behind the gallon of milk. He pulled a dirty glass from the sink, rinsed it out, then filled it with the soda and handed it to John. John tipped the glass to Mamma's lips and she slurped some into her mouth. The soda dribbled out the corners of her mouth, down to the neck of her muumuu.

The operator said she would not hang up until they arrived. "How is she doing?" the operator asked. "Is she cold? Can she move, or stand?" When Clyde finally saw the flashing red lights moving up the trailer park road, he excitedly told the operator they had arrived, then thanked her and hit the END button on the phone, disconnecting the call.

John and Clyde were still in their underwear. John ran to his room, threw on the ratty pair of sweatpants with the hole in the leg that exposed his beautiful, muscled thighs and an equally tattered tee-shirt.

Then Clyde dressed in the clothes he had on earlier in the night. The same jeans and tight tee-shirt Evan had so lovingly peeled from him before covering Clyde's chest with his hungry, kissing mouth.

Clyde flung open the trailer door and waved the EMTs inside. There were two of them, a husky man with thick, tattoo-covered forearms and a small, very pretty woman. She had long, blond hair pulled back in a ponytail that swayed from one shoulder to the other as she ran up the steps to the trailer door. John stood straighter when he saw her, sucked in the gut he did not have. The woman was carrying a large, plastic box that looked to Clyde like something one would carry their fishing tackle with. When she opened it though, it wasn't full of hooks and feathery lures, but syringes, cotton pads and small glass jars of clear liquids with names like Dipenhyrdramine and Epinephrine emblazoned across the labels.

"Mrs. Chute? My name is Sherilyn," the woman said, dropping to her knees beside Mamma. "I understand you are having chest pains. Is that right?"

"Yes. I think it's my hah-t. It hurts bad."

"Where does it hurt?"

"He-ah," Mamma replied, grabbing her ample left breast. "And down my left ah-m."

"Have you had this pain before?" Sherilyn opened the tackle box, pulled out a syringe and one of the the small medicine vials.

"No. I ain't never felt nothing like this before. What's that in the bottle? I just took some aspirin. My John gave it to me." Mamma looked over at John and Clyde. Clyde could see the fear in her eyes. They were wide, darting over John, himself and the male EMT, then flash briefly over the woman before starting back at John again.

"That's good," Sherilyn said in a smooth, calm voice. She wasn't panicked. The calmness of her voice suggested Mamma should not panic either. Clyde wondered if that voice was taught in EMT classes. "This is Streptokinase, it's to help break up any clots in your arteries, if you have any. This, along with the aspirin you took earlier, may prevent any damage to your heart, if you indeed have had a heart attack."

"You don't know if that's what it is?"

"No, ma'am. We are going to take you to the hospital and they will do tests there to find out exactly what happened. The Streptokinase is just a precaution." Sherilyn pushed the needled syringe into the rubber cap on the top of the bottle, tipped them upside down while pulling back on the syringe plunger, then slid the needle free. She held it in her mouth like a dog with his favorite bone as she wiped Mamma's arm with an alcohol wipe, then plunged the needle into her arm.

"Ooh," Mamma squealed at the quick stab.

The husky male EMT looked down at Mamma, then glanced back at the door they had come through. He pulled John aside and spoke to him in a whisper low enough so even Clyde, standing just six feet away, could not hear. John nodded his head at whatever the man was saying, then they walked out the door. The EMT went to the ambulance and John headed in the opposite direction, to the garage. Clyde watched through the window as the single bare bulb hanging from the garage ceiling came on and John pulled the tool box he kept under his weight bench, pulled a few items from it, turned the light out again and marched back up the short staircase to the front door. He opened the door and motioned for Clyde to join him outside. In his hand, bunched together like a bouquet of flowers, was a crowbar and an old wooden-handled hammer. He handed the crowbar to Clyde.

"We need to get the front door off," he said. "Mamma might not be able to fit even with the frame gone, but we need to try this before cutting a hole in the wall."

"Okay," Clyde said. This was going to devastate Mamma, he knew. She had been embarrassed about her weight and Clyde assumed she never went outside because she didn't want people in the park to see how big she had gotten. Or, at least he liked to think that's what the problem was. Deep down he knew, though, she hadn't gone outside in so long because she couldn't go outside. She had grown too large to fit through the door. He had not been oblivious to her size. But, like Mamma, had deluded himself into thinking it hadn't been a physical complication that kept her indoors, but a psychological one. The truth was she was just too fat to get through the door.

John hooked the claw end of the hammer into the thin vinyl strips of decorative molding surrounding the door and pulled them from the outside wall. They came away with a rumbling screech that reminded Clyde of fingernails on a chalkboard. He felt a cold shiver run

up his spine. John opened the door, stepped inside and began working on the wooden molding inside the door. Mamma looked over at
him, her head twisting as far around as it would move. The bulging
folds of fat in her neck looking to Clyde like a pack of the cheap hot
dogs they had by the dozens in the freezer. Sherilyn had the rubber-
tipped ends of a stethoscope in her ears, the cold, round amplifier on
Mamma's chest.

"What are you doing, John?" Mamma asked. John ignored her. He
wouldn't answer because, Clyde was sure, this embarrassed John as
much as it did Mamma. When he and Clyde began pulling the wood
framing of the door from out of the wall, Mamma understood just
what they were doing. "Oh," she muttered and there was a sob buried
deep in that single word.

Mamma began to cry. A low, quiet sob she tried to shield from
Clyde and John, but they noticed anyway and said nothing. They continued to work pulling the door and its frame from the front of the
trailer. Clyde tossed the narrow wooden planks of framing onto the
ground behind the steps railing, then he and John lifted the door and
walked it over to the garage. They leaned it against the garage wall,
then came back to the trailer and sat on the steps.

The tattooed EMT climbed from the ambulance, approached
Clyde and John. The name badge sewn to his shirt said his name
was Cody. It seemed a small, gentle name for such an imposing man,
Clyde thought.

"I called in for a larger stretcher. I don't know if we will be able to
get her out of there, but if we can, she won't fit on the bed we have,"
Cody said, keeping his voice to a low mumble. Lights had come on
in some of the neighboring trailers and faces, puffy-eyed and curious,
gazed out windows. Curtains held back with one hand while, in some
of the very early risers, coffee mugs gripped in the other.

Clyde went into the trailer to start a pot of coffee and to check
on Mamma. There would be no more sleep for anyone tonight. He
glanced at the clock on the broken microwave oven. It was 3:15 in the
morning. In another hour they would have been heading off to the
woods to work. He wondered if Evan was awake yet. He and Dale
would need to be told there would be no work for them today. Then
as though John could hear his thoughts, he stepped into the kitchen,

picked up the phone and dialed Dale's number. Clyde could hear Dale's voice erupt on the line. John quickly pulled the handset from his ear, then a loud beep echoed from the phone. The answering machine had picked up. John left him a message detailing the situation, that they would be at the hospital today but, no matter what, would come back to work tomorrow. He didn't say it, but Clyde knew John could not afford to take more than one day off. No matter how sick he was or whatever might be happening at home, he could not be out of work for more than a single day.

When he was done, John handed the cordless receiver to Clyde. "Call Evan," he said, then walked back outside to wait with Cody for the larger stretcher.

"Hello?" Evan asked, his voice cautious to be receiving a phone call at this time of the morning.

"Hey, Evan," Clyde said and felt his heart beat a little faster at hearing Evan's voice. Even with the situation going on around him, he felt a smile curling his lips, a flutter in his belly. He knew there was something between them beyond the sex they had shared just seven hours ago.

At least, he felt something more.

"Clyde? What are you doing calling? What time is it? Three? We are going to see each other in a few hours and..." he paused.

Clyde felt his belly drop. He sounded almost angry that Clyde had called him. It was early, but he had been awake already. He answered on the first ring. *What the fuck do you mean by calling me so soon?* Clyde read between the lines in his voice. *We fooled around, that's it. Jesus Christ, if I had of known you were so fucking needy I never would have...*

"Sorry. I'm still half asleep. Let me start over," Evan said, pushing the thoughts out of Clyde's head. "Clyde," he continued, "it's good to hear you voice again. This is the best wake-up call I've ever gotten."

Clyde started to reply, but his voice cracked in his throat. He wanted to tell Evan that it had only been a few hours since they were together on his couch, Clyde's fingers combing the thick fur on Evan's belly and he couldn't get the thought of him out of his head. He wanted to tell Evan how much he wanted to hold him again. To feel their bare bodies pressed against one another again. To taste him and not just his cock, though that was heavenly, but his whole being. He wanted to drink him as though he were a mountain spring, clean and pure. He wanted to... he wanted to love him.

"We're not going out to work today," he finally managed to say. "You have the day off."

"Really? Why?"

"Something happened to Mamma. The ambulance is here right now. They are taking her to the hospital."

"Oh Clyde, what happened? Is she alright?" Evan asked, real concern rippling his voice. A worried shiver. "Are you okay?"

"I'm alright. We think it's her heart. I think we are going to be at the hospital all day. But John wanted me to tell you that we *will* be working tomorrow."

"Okay. Should I call Dale, let him know?"

"No, John already talked to him," Clyde said and a quick question passed through him. Why had John told him to call Evan? Why hadn't he done it himself? John was the boss and he had made that very clear on more than one occasion. Informing Evan that there would be no work today was his responsibility that normally he would proudly have done. But he didn't. He wanted Clyde to do it. Was he still mad at Evan for the comments he had made that first day? They had apologized to one another so it didn't seem likely that...

Why had John apologized? He had only been honestly sorry once and that was for knocking out Clyde's front tooth. He threw sorrys to Darlene occasionally, but they were as light and fragile as popcorn. But there had seemed to be genuine regret in his voice when he apologized to Evan that day.

"Do you want me to meet you at the hospital?" Evan asked.

"No, you don't have to do that. Thank you though."

"You sure? I give great moral support."

"I'm sure you do," Clyde said and felt a laugh rush past his lips. "You don't have to come if you don't want to. We will probably have to work all day Saturday and Sunday to make up for today. This might be your only day off and you don't want to spend it in the hospital, do you?"

"I don't hear a no. I don't hear you telling me to stay away," Evan said and Clyde could hear the smile in his voice. He was not asking Evan to be with him at the hospital, but was not ordering him not to either.

"No, you don't hear that. You will never hear that from me. I would never ask you to leave me alone."

"Good. I'll see you there. I'll bring plenty of change for the vending machine."

Chapter 11
Like More Than Like

Clyde hated the hospital. He hated its cold sterility, the ultra clean stink of antiseptics and industrial cleaners. He hated its obsessive cleanliness, as though it were attempting to eradicate every trace of the people here, of the lives that began and ended here. He preferred the rich, earthy smells of the forest. The air cleaned by a summer rain, droplets pattering his shoulders as it fell from the branches above his head. He liked the feel of the soil beneath his feet. Crisp and dry in the summer, slick with melted snow in the spring. He was a man who lived outside in the natural world. The hospital was an indoor place where everything, even the temperature, was controlled. Everything but the fear he felt for his mother.

He sat in the waiting room, hands clasped, bent at the waist, staring at the perfect, freshly waxed floor tiles. John paced back and forth in front of him. Marching like a sentry, nervously stopping every few minutes to drop in the chair opposite Clyde, tap his boots against the floor until he could no longer tolerate staying seated and jump back up to pace some more. He was like a shark, moving constantly, swimming through the clean, quiet waiting area not looking for food, but some word that their mother was going to be all right.

"John, how is she?" Darlene walked into the waiting room and Clyde looked up, startled. She was carrying a cardboard tray with three coffees and a bag of pastries from the bakery in town.

"Hey, Darlene," John said. He took the food and drinks from her, set them on a small table stacked with old magazines and wrapped his arms around her. "How did you find out?"

"Small town," she replied, then added, "Dale called me."

"I forgot how much you Pruitts love to gossip."

"So, was it her heart?"

"Yeah, she had a heart attack. Cardiac Infarction, I guess is what the rag-head doctor called it. Doesn't sound serious like that, does it? Infarction. Sounds like she has gas or that she shit herself. They're admitting her. We're just waiting for a room to open up, then we can see her."

Darlene looked over at Clyde. "How are you doing, Hon?"

"I'm fine. Thank you." Clyde smiled at her, then closed his eyes again. The exhausted fog had smothered his brain again, almost closing him off from the rest of the world. He needed sleep and lots of it.

"Poor baby is beat," John laughed. "He was out half the night again. Whoring around I bet."

"I wasn't whoring around," Clyde said, keeping his eyes closed as he spoke. "That's your job, John."

"Who's whoring around?"

Clyde's eyes snapped open like window shades in a cartoon. He could almost feel them spinning around and around a spring-loaded rod in his head. It was Evan's voice. He looked to the archway into the waiting room and saw him standing there. He had brought three coffees as well.

"John is. As usual," Darlene joked. "Hey, cousin."

"Hey," he said, then turned his attention to Clyde. "How is your mother doing?" His voice had dropped its humor and filled with sudden concern. Clyde not only heard the worry in his voice, but saw it in his eyes as well. Evan had never met Mamma though, so the concern must be for him. He hoped it was because he suspected if the roles were reversed and it was Evan's mother in the hospital, Clyde would be frantic with worry for him.

Evan noticed the coffee and bag of pastries Darlene had brought, set his own tray next to them on the table, then sat beside Clyde. "Is she doing okay, or..."

"She's fine. Well, she will be fine, they think."

"Good. And how are you?"

"I'm still conscious. Tired as hell, but still awake."

"Drink this." Evan stood, grabbed one of the cups of coffee he had brought and handed it to Clyde. "It'll perk you up."

Not as much as you do, Clyde thought, then thanked Evan out loud. He drank the coffee, but no amount of caffeine could shake the tired feeling from his bones. Nothing but sleep.

The day crew began to filter into the small hospital. Clyde watched as dozens of men and women in scrubs and rubber Crocs or clean, white nurse's shoes rushed past the waiting room. "Thank you for waiting here with me," Clyde said in a voice so low he hoped John, just eight feet away, could not hear. "You didn't have to do this, you know."

"Yes, I did," Evan said. The finality in his voice spoke volumes to Clyde. He not only had insisted on the phone earlier that he would be here with him, he needed to be here. Giving Clyde the support he needed at this time was as important to Evan as it was for Clyde in receiving it. He cared about Clyde.

"What are you girls whispering about over there?" John asked.

"I was just saying what a cute couple you two are. When are you going to make an honest man out of him, Darlene?" Evan replied.

Darlene let out a chuckle, but didn't reply. John rolled his eyes.

Finally, a nurse approached and informed them that Mamma would be going to the Intensive Care Unit in half an hour. They could visit for a few minutes once she was settled.

"Let's go for a walk while we wait," Evan said as he stood. Clyde followed him out of the waiting room and down the hall. They passed a few employees who nodded or smiled at them, then Evan ducked down a corridor that ended with a large metal door. A bright red bio-hazard sign blazed over the door, letting everyone know to keep out unless authorized. The hall was abandoned, it seemed to Clyde. Evan leaned against the wall, took Clyde's hand in his. Clyde nervously glanced over his shoulder, out at the busy, vibrant hospital. People passed by the entrance to the hall, but no one noticed them. No one really cared.

"I had a good time last night," Evan said.

"I did, too."

"You want to do it again? Soon? Maybe, you can stay the night next time."

"I'd like that. I think it would be nice, waking up next to you."

Clyde looked into Evan's eyes. The left eye had strayed slightly, but was more focused directly ahead than he had seen it before. It seemed like Evan was making a conscious effort to keep both eyes focused on him. "I... I like you, Clyde," Evan said.

"I like you, too."

"No, I..." Evan paused, struggled with his words a moment, then continued. "I really like you. We've only known each other, what... two days? Two days, and I can't stop thinking about you. When I bought that *Battlelines* game Monday night, I wasn't thinking how much fun it would be to play. I thought about how much fun it would be to play the game with you. When you came over last night, I never suspected that what happened between us would actually happen. I hoped it would and when you kissed me... I knew I would never have a happier moment in my life. Even if I lived to be a thousand years old, I would never feel as good, as special as that."

Clyde felt himself grow a little dizzy from what Evan was saying. Lightheaded. He made Evan feel special? How was that possible? How could he, a nobody, make someone as wonderful as Evan feel anything more than a casual interest? But he had. Clyde could feel a smile start to spread over his face. He felt the smile growing inside him as well.

"After you left though, I could still smell you on my clothes. I wanted you back there with me. I missed you just ten minutes after you were gone from my driveway. I lay in bed wide awake until just an hour before you called me this morning, with my shirt pressed against my face because I could smell you on it.

"My grandmother says that people our age are more... I don't know, susceptible to emotions than others. She told me once that we haven't grown cynical yet. We haven't grown that hard shell that older people have. Well, I don't want that shell. I like feeling this way, even though it's kind of... painful."

Painful? Clyde wondered if it was the same pain he felt just looking at Evan. A wonderful ache deep down in his insides that made his belly cramp and his heart beat like a maniac drumming his chest, but it felt so damned good as it tore him apart. Could it be that kind of pain?

"I don't know what I feel for you," Evan continued. "I think I love you, but I'm not really sure what love is. You read about it books and hear it in songs and being in love sounds so wonderful, like walking on the clouds. But, if love is what I'm feeling for you, it hurts. There is the cloud thing when we are together. When I can see you, touch you, I feel like a god. Like I can take on the world and nothing will hurt me as long as you are there beside me. But when you're not there? It hurts so fucking much I want to die."

Tears had formed in his eyes as he spoke. They ran down his cheeks and collected on his chin. Clyde reached out and wiped them away with his thumb, then leaned in and kissed him. A group of young nursing students walked by the entrance to the hall as Clyde and Evan kissed. The students let out a loud giggle, then moved on. Clyde heard them, but didn't care. He wasn't ashamed to be with Evan, he was proud. Evan wasn't the lucky one in this, he was.

"I like you, Clyde. I like you more than like."

"What does that mean?" Clyde said, his lips hovering just an inch or so from Evan's mouth.

"There are, um... four things a person can feel for another. Hate, dislike, like and love. I don't know if I love you. I probably do, but I've never been in love before so I don't really know. I know I more than like you though. So, maybe what I feel is somewhere between like and love. Extreme like, I guess."

Evan liked him more than like. It was an odd sentiment, but it fit what Clyde felt for Evan as well. Evan was correct about the other thing, as well. If this was love, then the songs had it all wrong. Love fucking hurt.

Clyde took Evan's face in his hands, then leaned in and licked the tears away. "Please don't cry anymore," he said. "I don't know why you like me. I really can't figure it out."

"Clyde, you..." Evan started. Clyde removed his hands from Evan's cheeks and set his left palm over Evan's mouth.

"Please," Clyde said, "let me say this."

Evan nodded his head that he would and twisted his fingers in front of the hand covering his mouth, as though he were turning a key in a lock over his lips.

Clyde continued, "I've never met anyone that makes me feel the way you make me feel. When I'm with you I feel like I'm going crazy. I want to touch you everywhere, every inch of your body at once. I want to press myself against you and feel your heart beat against my own. I want to enter you and see the world through your eyes. Maybe then, I might understand what you see in me. I want to know everything about you. I want to *know* you just like I know myself.

"Whatever I did to deserve you was the smartest thing I ever did. I can't stand *not* being with you. When I left your place last night, I wanted to turn around and go back to you even before I got off your road. Saying goodbye was so fucking hard, even though I knew it was only for a few hours. But, even a few minutes hurts like hell when I'm not with you.

"I feel crazy when I'm with you, but I feel like I'm dying when I'm not."

It was just after ten in the morning when Clyde and John arrived back at the trailer. They stumbled from the truck, John dragging his feet up to the trailer door, Clyde so exhausted everything in his peripheral vision was growing dark, like the sun was setting, but only for him. John forgot about the door and nearly pulled it on top of him. "Son of a bitch," he screamed and kicked it while still holding onto the doorknob. He left a large dent in the bottom corner.

Clyde stepped into the trailer and John followed him in, leaving the door leaning against the outside wall. "I'll get us something to eat," Clyde said, pulled a couple cans of ravioli from the cupboard, dumped them in a pan and spun the burner knob to low. John went to the garage, came back with a fistful of nails and began fixing the door. When he was done with that, the food was hot and they sat and ate.

"I hope that rag-head doctor knows what he is doing," John said, spoon dripping with tomato sauce hovering over his bowl.

"Actually I think he is Indian, not Middle Eastern."

"So?" John blurted, slamming his fist clutching the spoon onto the table. Tomato sauce sprayed across the room, nearly covering Clyde. "I don't give no fuck where he's from. He ain't American, that's all that matters."

"Alright. I'm sorry."

John looked at the mess he had made, grabbed the small towel hanging from the oven door and wiped the sauce from the table. "No, you ain't got nothing to be sorry for," he said, his voice surprisingly gentle. "I don't mean to yell at you. I'm just worried, that's all."

"I know. I am too, but you heard what he said. Mamma is going to be okay. We need to get rid of this shit food around here, though. Buy some fresh stuff."

They weren't really sure how to do that. The groceries John bought each month with Mamma's food stamps might be junk, but it was the only food he understood. The produce aisle was as foreign to him as Mamma's doctor.

After Dr. Sing made it clear to them what needed to change in their house for Mamma's well being, the hospital social worker made a visit to Mamma's hospital room. She explained to Mamma about the low-income charity program the hospital had for those without the money to pay for treatment.

MaineCare would pay for a great deal of the bill, but not all of it. The hospital program would try to take care of the rest.

John grumbled at first. He didn't like the idea of charity, no matter how needed it was. But when the social worker explained that their portion of the bill could easily be in the thousands of dollars, perhaps as much as five thousand, John relented and told her to go ahead with the paperwork.

Clyde finished eating, dumped the bowl in the sink without rinsing it, then went to his room. He pulled the curtains closed, blocking out the sun and heat, stripped to his boxers and climbed into bed. He didn't think he could keep his eyes open another second and was starting to drift off to sleep when he heard John come into the room.

"I thought you might want some company," John said.

"Sure. I'd love it," Clyde said and pulled the covers back. He wanted sleep more than anything, but had hoped John would come to him. He was scared about losing Mamma. He knew John was as well and he also knew that the fear he felt was far different than what John must be feeling. John had been old enough to really know their father when he died. He could remember him vividly and what it felt like to lose him. Mamma was their only living parent, but at least Clyde had John if things went bad for Mamma. John would have no one but Clyde, the brother he had helped raise like a son.

John was in his briefs, shining white in the dark. He slid in the bed and turned on his side spooning Clyde. The hard muscles of John's chest and belly massaged Clyde and the thick dark hair covering John felt like little fingers on his tired body. Clyde moaned in response to John's touch. It felt good. It felt like he was safe here with his brother's body holding him, protecting him. He pushed himself back against him, felt John's body dig into him.

Clyde thought of Evan and wondered if he would feel this good pressed against his back. He thought he probably would. He would even like it better, he bet. John let out a little snore and Clyde felt the wet press of lips to his neck. A shiver ran up his spine.

John was sleeping. Clyde could hear his steady breathing. His slow, regular pulse beating into his back. The steady rhythm slowly drew Clyde to the edge of sleep. He hovered there, clung to the edge of wakefulness. Then John's hand moved up onto Clyde's hip, slid down over his belly and pressed into the rigid stand of Clyde's erection. He hadn't even realized he was hard until John touched it. That touch though, could not let him forget it. It throbbed and flexed, sending mad thoughts and desires into Clyde's head. He wondered, with John asleep, how far he could go with him before he woke. Could he get John out of his underwear? Could he play with him until he was as hard as Clyde now was? Could he finally get a taste of it, push his brother's cock down into his throat before John woke, confused. then angry? He would be angry too, Clyde knew this. But would it be worth it?

Finally, John released him, rolled over onto his other side and the snore became more regular, steadier.

Clyde drifted off to sleep, not thinking of John's hands that had just been in his lap, but Evan and his confession to him back at the hospital. He said he might be in love with Clyde. And Clyde thought he might be in love with Evan right back.

Chapter 12
Who Do You Want to Be?

Clyde woke with a scream struggling to claw its way from his throat. Sweat dampened his body. His armpits, chest and back were slick with the salty moisture that trickled down into his boxers, making the thin cotton material cling to him like plastic wrap. His eyes snapped open.

Where am I? his mind nearly screamed aloud. He saw the sunlight coming in through the thin curtains over his head. He saw the bedside table with the electric alarm clock and the lamp with the ripped shade. He was in his room. He was safe and in his own bed. The quick thumping of his heart still beat-beat-beat, but was beginning to slow. Clyde could feel himself begin to calm. His breathing was becoming more regular. The quick, burpy pants, the furious intakes and exhales slowed to a more regular rhythm.

John lay under him. Clyde's head was on his brother's belly and John's slow, steady breathing nearly lulled him back to sleep. Then he remembered what woke him. He remembered the dream.

He had been in the section of woods where he, John, Evan and Dale had been working all week. His dream self could smell the comforting rush of sawdust, old leaves and his own sweat. He loved the smells. The aroma of nature and hard work. He could feel the early morning dew rising up from the forest floor to dampen his boots and pant legs. Felt the moisture on his face as it dropped from the branches over his head.

He stepped into a clearing and saw someone lying on the forest floor. He saw the long expanses of flesh, and knew the person was nude. Excitement fluttered inside him. He stepped closer. The person lying on a bed of pine needles was a man. Clyde could see the cock, draped over the thin hip. The man was hairy, very hairy. Pine needles and decomposing leaves weaved in and out of the hair on the man's chest and belly as though they had been carefully placed there. Like they had been meticulously woven into the hairy carpet.

Clyde took another step closer to the man. There was something familiar about him. The look of his body, the beautiful circumcised cock lying there waiting to be toyed with. Then Clyde realized who it was. It was Evan.

What is Evan doing lying naked on the ground? Clyde thought. *Is he...* but he wouldn't finish the thought. He couldn't allow himself to even think the word. Dead. He stepped even closer, hoping to see Evan's chest rise and fall with his breaths. *He has to be breathing. He has to be okay.* A mud handprint covered Evan's left shoulder. The hair flowing up from his chest, clumped with the filth. It was a large hand that had touched him there, that had gripped his shoulder. It was the same size as John's hand.

He saw Evan's chest move with his breathing and Clyde let out a long, steady exhale. He hadn't realized he had been holding his breath.

John appeared then. He, like Evan, was nude as well. His hard, muscular body shimmered with sweat as he knelt between Evan's legs and lifted them, exposing the furry, muscled slabs of Evan's butt. John was erect, the thick foreskin of his cock pulled back revealing the fat mushroom head. He grabbed his cock at the base and pushed it into Evan. Evan moaned a deep pleasured grunt as John pushed himself inside him. John shoved himself balls deep in the first thrust, tearing into Evan with his long, fat cock.

Evan turned his head towards Clyde. A laugh poured out of him. A happy, joyful laugh as John pounded harder, deeper into him.

"Who do you want to be?" Evan had asked, his voice echoing through the pines. Reverberating against the trees. "Who do you want to be, Clyde?"

That's when Clyde had woken up, his head on John's belly. Now he studied the thick trail of hair tracing down John's abdomen into the confines of his white — *well, mostly white* — briefs stretched out before Clyde like a highway. The mound of his crotch, like one of the great hills surrounding Devon, hovered there in Clyde's line of sight. It beckoned to him. *"Climb me,"* it said.

Clyde wondered if he was still dreaming as the mound began to move. It shifted and rumbled as a fast quake rippled through it. He could see the outline of John's cock begin to slither under the cotton material, like a snake moving through tall grass. It slowly pushed its way out from under the elastic band, facing Clyde. The foreskin sealed over the head in a thin, flat line, looking like a pair of lips wearing a grimace. Then they separated, exhaling a breath of vinegary, unwashed cock. Clyde inhaled the hot, musky smell and felt his own cock growing hard even with the weird, surreal situation.

The foreskin lips spoke. "Touch me," they muttered. "Taste me."

He wanted to touch it. He wanted to taste it. He had wanted this for as long as he could remember. Clyde moved in closer so his own lips brushed the foreskin lips. He slid his tongue from his mouth and reached for his brother's cock with it. It made contact, but when he looked down, saw that a small, thin tongue had flickered out from John's cock and that was what his tongue was touching. The foreskin tongue was split, like a snake's. He was French kissing John's cock.

Clyde woke, really woke this time. He was in his bedroom, in his bed. John was lying under him. Clyde's head on John's belly. The cotton mound of John's crotch hovering there before Clyde's eyes just like in his dream. It didn't move, though. A snake cock did not slide out and flick a forked tongue at him. He was back in the real world, bathed in sweat, his heart hammering in his chest like a jackhammer.

The dream began to fade, to drift away like a morning mist rising from a cool lake. He tried to catch it, but it slipped through his fingers. Evan was in it, wasn't he? There was something about a handprint. A mud handprint and John in the woods and... and it was gone, leaving only a weak feeling of unease and six little words.

"Who do you want to be?" Who had said it? Was it Evan? John?

Clyde looked ahead, down John's thick pleasure trail to the white mountain ahead of him. The mound of gorgeous cock and balls wrapped in cotton. John's cock and balls. There was no dream anymore. The point of his decade-long obsession drew every ounce of his attention. His head rose and fell with John's breath. John's belly moving like waves on the ocean, Clyde's head, the ship that carried him towards the snow-capped mountain of John's crotch in the horizon.

Clyde lifted his hand and slowly, so slowly as to not wake John, set it on the mound. He could feel the fat orbs of John's testicles, held tight by the briefs, but loose in the wrinkled, furry sack. He traced his fingers up to the cock, traced the length of it. Felt it pulse and flex in response to his touch. It began to grow, to stretch along John's hip, inflate with the warm blood pouring into it.

Clyde could smell the sex coming from it. The hot stink of sweat and musk. And when the thick head pushed its way out from under the elastic band, the acidic vinegar stench of his dirty cock swam into Clyde's face, stinging his eyes and making his mouth water. The head was pointed directly at him, the foreskin rolled back enough for the glistening moisture trickling from the piss-slit to reflect the dim light of the room.

He wanted to taste it. Feel it grow rigid in his mouth. He wanted to impale himself on his brother's long, fat pole. To feel it thrust down his throat. To push down into him further than any had ever been. He wanted to choke on it, feel it split him like an ax blade through a chunk of pine. Feel it tear him apart, then afterwards, John would reassemble him. Like piecing together a jigsaw puzzle.

The only way to do all this was to free his brother's penis from the stained underwear. Release it from its cotton prison. Clyde slid his fingers under the elastic band, his thumb briefly making contact with the head peeking out at him, like a watchful eye. It rose involuntarily at the touch, hovered over the thatch of pubic hair, the underwear band stretching, then dropped back down again. He pulled on the cloth, lifting it two, three, four inches into the air. It was all there in front of him now, down in the dark underwear cave. Everything he wanted since he turned twelve and discovered that his penis was for more than just peeing.

He hooked his thumb into the elastic band and pulled the briefs back. Hooked them under John's scrotum, leaving John's beautiful, magnificent, glorious genitals naked and exposed for him to worship.

"You having fun down there?" John's voice broke the quiet of the room.

Clyde's balls shriveled up to his chest. Fear made his head swim drunkenly and his stomach tightened to a hard knot. He felt sweat suddenly dampen his forehead and armpits.

"What?" Clyde moaned, feigning sleep, as though John's sudden voice had just woken him. He inhaled a quick catch of John's sex smell, then lifted his head from John's belly. He rubbed his eyes, squinted them to continue the illusion he had woken only seconds ago instead of minutes and gave his brother an innocent smile. "Good morning," he said, even though he knew perfectly well, it was the late afternoon.

John pulled his underwear back up, covering himself and rose from the bed. He glared at Clyde, as if gauging the honesty of his act. He opened his mouth to say something, but no sound came from him. He clamped his mouth shut again and stalked out of the room. "Go make some coffee," he ordered, his heavy footsteps stomping towards the bathroom.

Clyde crawled from the bed, his erection blaring out through the hole in his boxers. He stuffed it back inside, then walked out to the kitchen to make the coffee John had demanded.

When the kitchen filled with the rich scent of fresh coffee John appeared in the doorway. He sat at the table, still wearing just his underwear. He stared at Clyde as Clyde rinsed two mugs from the pile of dirty dishes in the sink, set them on the counter and pulled the powdered creamer and sugar bowl from the cupboard.

"What were you doing in there?" John asked.

"Where?" Clyde replied, not looking at John. He couldn't make eye contact with him. John would see the fear in his eyes and whatever lies he would have to come up with to cover-up what he had just done would be moot. John would know the truth if he saw the terror in Clyde's eyes.

"You know what the fuck I'm talking about. Don't fucking play games with me, Clyde." John rose from the table, took a step towards him, John's fists flexing and releasing again and again. The thick, blue veins running up his arms bulged under the skin.

Clyde backed into the counter. He could feel the heat of the drip coffee maker at his back as the decanter filled with the hot brew. "I was dreaming, John. I was just having a dream. I didn't know what I was doing," he whined, fear quivering his voice. John was going to hit him. He could feel the rage building in his brother as John stepped closer. John was furious and he might not stop at one punch, he might let it go on to two, ten, twenty. He might not stop until Clyde was bloody, broken, barely alive. That is, if John stopped even then. "Please, John," he begged.

"You want this, don't you?" John said, grabbing his own crotch, the thick fistful of cock and balls straining against the piss-stained underwear. "You've always wanted this. Ever since you was a kid, you tried to sneak a peek at this, haven't you? I seen you staring at me, wanting me. I let you see it a few times, too. Yeah, nothing more fun than teasing a little pussy-boy like you. I let you see what you couldn't have. It made you crazy, didn't it? Made you want me even more. You're just like those bitches at Sparky's. Sniffing around, wanting all this man inside them. Is that what you want? You want this cock in your little asshole? You want me to stretch you out like an old, worn cunt?"

Clyde felt his chin begin to quiver. Tears filled his eyes, but he couldn't, wouldn't let them fall. He was more scared now than he had ever been. Scared of John, scared of himself for what he had almost done in the bedroom. John stepped closer to him. Clyde could smell his breath in his face, feel the heat of his body as John's naked chest touched his own. He felt John's cock, now stiffened to the point it strained against the underwear, press against Clyde's own flaccid crotch.

"It's time you got what you wanted for so long. You deserve it. It's time you knew what it feels like to have my cock tear into you." John grabbed Clyde by the throat, spun him around and threw him into one of the kitchen chairs around the cheap Formica table. He stepped in front of him, yanked down his underwear and thrust his cock in Clyde's face.

Clyde stared at it. The engorged, fat, purple head hovered before his eyes. The raw sex stink flowed from it, filled his sinuses and, much to Clyde's disgust, made his mouth water. He glanced up at John's face. There was hot rage in his eyes. A violent anger that forced his pupils down to tiny specks in a hazel sea. Clyde kept his mouth firmly shut, refusing John to enter him.

"Suck it!" John bellowed.

Clyde wouldn't. He backed from it, pushed back into the chair as deeply as he could.

Who do you want to be, he heard Evan from his dream say.

"You wanted this, now take it," John said. He was right, Clyde had wanted it. When he was younger, he had wanted John so badly it hurt. Now though—with the object of years of sexual desire just inches from his face—Clyde realized he didn't want John and never really had. John was his brother, but also a man who raised him as a father would. He was his closest friend for most of his life. All of his life actually. Until Clyde met Evan.

Who do you want to be?

He didn't want to be the Evan in his dream, getting fucked by John. He didn't want to be the sort of man who had sex with his own brother. He didn't want to be that sort of man who *wanted* sex with his own brother.

He wanted to be a man whose love was returned the same way he gave it. A man who would feel no shame in who he fucked and was fucked by. A man who was proud of the man he wanted. Like the pride he felt earlier at the hospital, when the nursing students had seen him and Evan kissing in the hallway.

Who did he want to be?

He wanted to be the man he already was. A man who was loved by and in love with Evan.

"You fucking faggot, suck my cock!" John grabbed Clyde's face with one hand and tried to pry his mouth open. The other hand wrapped around Clyde's neck and John tried to pull him into his cock. "You wanted it. Now do it!"

Clyde brought his hands up and pushed John's hands away. "Enough!" he screamed.

John came at him again. He grabbed him by the neck again and dug his fingers between Clyde's lips, finally forcing his mouth open. "You're gonna take this cock. If I have to..."

But John couldn't finish the sentence because Clyde *really* had enough. He knocked John's hands away from him, jumped from the chair and pushed John back into the counter. John's elbow struck the coffee maker, pushing it into the wall behind it. The decanter slipped from the heated base enough to teeter on the lip of the machine, then it dropped onto the counter. It didn't shatter, but coffee poured over the counter and splashed against John's bare back. He let out a loud yelp and jumped away from the wall. "Motherfucker!" he screamed.

"Enough," Clyde said again, softer this time. He set the glass pot back in its base, the plunger that stopped the flow of coffee into the decanter opened and started filling it again. He grabbed a handful of paper towels from the rack under the cupboard, wet them and touched the paper cloth to John's back. John tried to pull away, but Clyde held onto his shoulder.

"Stop squirming. Let me see how bad this is," Clyde said and John did as told. There was a red patch of skin on John's lower back, where the coffee had splashed him. A minor burn, nothing to worry about. "You'll live," he said and tossed the soggy paper in the trash.

Clyde looked into John's eyes. The rage was gone. John quickly turned from him. His cock was still hanging out of his underwear. The flash of pain from the coffee had deflated his anger as well as his dick. He pulled the briefs back up where they belonged. "I... I'm so... I don't know what came over me," John said, his back still turned to him.

Clyde could hear a waver in John's voice, as though he were fighting tears, or had already lost the battle. He had gone too far, and he knew it. But, so had Clyde. He had been doing just what John thought he had been in that bed. He had been attempting to, at the very least, molest John in his sleep. At the most, rape him. How far would he have gotten if John hadn't woken and stopped him? "I'm sorry, John," he said.

"I... I..." John stammered, never turning to look at him. "We have to get dressed to go see Mamma." John walked out of the kitchen and down the hall to his room.

Chapter 13
Working for the Weekend

John and Clyde went to the hospital and stayed with Mamma until visiting hours ended. The ride to the hospital and back home again were mostly silent ones, broken only by the occasional slurp of coffee from their travel mugs or John pointing out someone he knew from Sparky's. "There's Janice," he would announce, then give the horn a quick beep. "Marla!" Another quick honk, this one followed by a wave as he drove past.

When they arrived home again John turned on the television, settled onto the couch. Clyde went to his room, dug the last of his pot from the small metal can in his dresser and shared it with John. They smoked, watched the reality show with the big breasted porn star, then John said he was going to bed. Very few words had passed between them after the incident in the kitchen earlier.

John had scared Clyde badly, but not as much as Clyde had scared himself. Clyde had attempted to have sex with John while he slept. He had attempted to—*no, please don't say it, don't say the word*—rape his brother. He hadn't, but only because John woke and stopped him. Of course, he had the opportunity to have John immediately after and he had turned it down, but still...

Could I have stopped myself if John hadn't woken? Would I have gone through with it? Would I have crossed that line and become a person that would do something like that?

He hoped he wouldn't, but he couldn't say that with any surety. He would never again have the opportunity to prove to himself that he could resist the temptation. Not that he really wanted the opportunity.

Once John went to bed, Clyde called Evan. He needed to hear his voice again, needed to hear the... what? Love? Admiration? Whatever it was he needed to know he was not a monster. He needed to hear that he was worthy of whatever it was Evan felt for him.

"How is your mother doing?" Evan asked.

"She's doing all right. She has to change her diet when she comes home. No more junk food in the house. No more fatty meats. Just lean chicken and vegetables."

"Oh, that kind of sucks. Well, if you want pizza or a bag of chips, you can always get some here."

"Is that an invite?"

"That's an open invitation," Evan said. "You can come over any time you want. You want to come over now? I'm going to bed right now, but I'll leave the door unlocked for you. You can just climb into bed with me."

"I'd love to, but..."

He wanted to tell him about what had happened between him and John. He wanted to hear Evan say that he understood. That he was still a good person, no matter what he might have done, or almost done. But, he couldn't. He couldn't tell him and probably wouldn't tell him. Not now at least. Maybe, some day in the far off future he might bring it up, but even then...

"I'd love to," he repeated, "but I'm beat. I'm going to go to bed, too. I'll see you in the morning."

"Okay. I'll see you out there in the pines."

Clyde started to hang the phone back on the wall when he heard Evan speak again. "Oh, and Clyde?"

"Yeah."

"I like you more than like."

Clyde grinned into the phone. "Yeah, I like you more than like, too." Then he hung up the phone and went to bed.

When they had their first break of the day at nine in the morning, John used Dale's cell phone to call the hospital to check on Mamma. She told him she was being discharged later in the afternoon. So, at three

John left work to pick her up and take her home. "Can you give Clyde a ride home?" he asked Dale.

"Of course," Dale quickly replied.

"Thank you." John turned to Clyde. "You're in charge. I'll see you back at home."

"What?" Clyde said, astounded at what John had just said. He was in charge? John never let him have any authority in the business. "I'm in charge?"

John said, quietly so Evan and Dale could not hear, "You are a man now. You proved that to me yesterday. You stood up to me, fought me. I respect that. It's time you had some responsibility."

Clyde opened his mouth to reply, then snapped it shut again. What could he say? How could he react to this new respect John had for him without gushing or sounding like a fool? "Well, I appreciate it, John. Thank you," he finally said.

"Maybe you might help me expand the business a little. Get a bigger contract with the paper mill. If we do, maybe we could hire these guys permanently. I can't do it alone, Clyde. I thought I could, but I need your smah-ts to make a better life for us."

"Sure. I'll do what I can to help you."

"No, you won't be helping me. It'll be for us. We will be pahtners. Equals."

They worked through the rest of the afternoon until the usual quitting time at six, then they piled into Dale's truck and headed home. The trailer park was on the east side of town, Dale and Evan lived on the west so Dale took Clyde home first. When they pulled in the driveway, John and Mamma had not arrived back yet. "You want to stay here with me for a while? I'll give you a ride home after Mamma and John get back," Clyde asked, his fingers secretly rubbing the small of Evan's back.

"Yeah, that will be cool."

They slid from the truck, Clyde thanked Dale for the lift, then they went into the trailer. Clyde immediately slipped his arms around Evan once the door was closed behind them. "I've been wanting to do this all day," he said and pulled at the buckles holding the overalls onto Evan's shoulders. The overalls dropped to the floor, Evan stepped out of them, then Clyde dropped his own pair to the floor.

They moved into Clyde's bedroom, kissing, touching one another as they traversed the narrow hallway.

In the bedroom Clyde pushed Evan onto the bed, straddled him and began tugging his clothes free until Evan lie naked, so beautifully naked, beneath him. Clyde stripped and they tangled themselves into one another. Arms, legs, whole bodies became one. They were both still hot and sweaty. Clumps of dirt clung to their bodies and a day's worth of hard work had matted the ample hair on Evan's body. They both smelled of old sweat and pine sap.

Clyde liked the smell. It was a manly smell. Raw and primal. He took Evan deep into his mouth, sucking on him until Evan began to squirm under him.

"Do you have any lube?" Evan asked.

"No. I think we have some vegetable oil, but..."

"That'll work. Go get it," Evan said.

"What for?"

"Just do it. Please." Clyde dutifully followed his request, ran out to the kitchen, his erection swaying from one hip to the other. He opened the cupboard, grabbed the oil and hurried back to the bedroom. Evan stood. "Lie down," he said.

Clyde settled on the bed, Evan pushed him down onto his back and straddled his hips. "What are you doing?" Clyde asked. His mouth had gone bone dry. He knew what Evan had in mind and the thought terrified him.

Evan was about to settle himself down onto Clyde's cock, an act that Clyde could see no physical pleasure in for Evan. This, he thought, was for Clyde's pleasure and Clyde's pleasure only. It would hurt Evan, just like the one time Clyde had slid an index finger in his own butt while masturbating. It had burned, like he was on fire down there, and that was just a finger. Clyde's cock was nearly as big around as his wrist. He is going to rip Evan.

"Are you sure you want to do this?" Clyde asked, hoping Evan would back out of it. He didn't want to hurt him, but he didn't want to deny Evan what he wanted.

"I'm sure," Evan replied and filled his palm with a pool of the oil. He coated Clyde's cock, then reached back and slid his slick fingers between his buttocks. He set the bottle on the table next to the electric alarm clock, then held Clyde's cock as he slowly pushed himself down on it.

As the head broke through the tight opening, Clyde nearly lost control. It was so incredibly warm and wet and the way Evan's body hugged him was... was... he didn't want to come yet. He wanted this to go on and on. Clyde turned his mind away from what was happening between them right then. He tried to think of anything to prevent himself from going over the edge already. He thought of Mamma's ugly, bruised legs. He remembered seeing the man stabbed to death at Sparky's last year. They had no effect. He was so close already he didn't think it was possible to reel it back in.

Then, he looked up and saw a clamp-toothed painful grimace on Evan's face. "Stop," Clyde said just as Evan had pushed himself all the way down on him. His entire cock was now engulfed in Evan's heat. "I don't want to do this if it hurts you."

"It hurts, but it feels good too," Evan said as he pulled himself up a bit, releasing Clyde's cock, then pushed back down, swallowing him again.

"Oh," Clyde moaned. "Are you sure?"

"Very," Evan said.

Clyde lifted his hips and pushed himself deeper into Evan. They began to work in tandem, Clyde pushing up as Evan forced himself down, their thrusts building in ferocity.

He watched the look of ecstasy on Evan's face. Eyes shut, bottom lip firmly clamped under his teeth. His hard cock slapped Clyde's belly with each downward thrust. Evan was in control of this. He was on top, riding Clyde. But now Clyde wanted the driver's seat. He wrapped his arms around Evan, pushed himself to his knees, never letting his cock pop from the hot, tight hole. Evan wrapped his arms around Clyde's neck and held on as Clyde turned and laid him on his back. He pulled Evan's legs up onto his shoulders and pushed himself all the way into Evan. His balls, low and heavy in the warm room, slapped against Evan's ass.

Evan squirmed beneath him, moaned, lifted his hips and pushed back against him. "Oh, it feels so good, Clyde. Fuck me."

Clyde pulled nearly all the way out of Evan, then slammed back into him again. The headboard banged against the wall. He watched the pleasure on Evan's face, heard the grunts and happy exclamations flowing from his panting mouth. The small twin bed squeaked and screamed as Evan lifted his hips and fucked Clyde back with the same force Clyde gave him.

He couldn't take much more. He was so close to coming now that nothing would prevent it. He could think of dead puppies and it still wouldn't hold off the inevitable. But he wanted Evan to come first. He reached between them and grabbed Evan's cock. The head was sticky with pre-come. He ran his oil slick thumb from the balls up to the head and felt it throb under his touch. He felt a response in the tight channel he was buried in, up to the balls, as it tightened even more around him. It felt like his cock was being strangled.

He couldn't stop the orgasm from coming now. He pressed his mouth against Evan's, their tongues mashed against one another as the explosive release rippled through him. Evan wrapped his arms around Clyde's back, pulled himself to form a seal between them. Clyde felt the hot wetness on his belly as Evan came with him. They screamed into one another's mouths as they came, not wanting to break the kiss even to catch their breaths.

As the waves of orgasm slowly subsided, Clyde slid from Evan. His cock, slick with vegetable oil and semen, plopped out from between Evan's hairy buttocks. Evan winced as it left him.

Clyde stood, pulled a dirty sock from under his bed and cleaned the come from Evan's belly, then wiped himself clean. He dropped the sock on the floor and climbed back on the bed. He slid his right arm under Evan and held him. He could feel the whispered beginnings of hair along Evan's shoulder blades. *By the time Evan is thirty*, Clyde thought, *his entire back will be covered in the same thick, dark hair that fills in his chest.* He hoped they would still be together when that happened.

Clyde settled in, set his head on Evan's chest. "Jesus, that was amazing." Evan said, running his fingers through Clyde's hair. Evan's voice was a hollow booming over the quick heartbeat that was beginning to slow as his body relaxed. "You fuck like a maniac, you know that?"

"I didn't hurt you, did I? I don't ever want to hurt you," Clyde said. It was true, he never wanted to hurt Evan. He knew that for many men their age, relationships generally didn't last too many years. But right at the moment, Clyde vowed to himself, he would do everything in his power to make sure that never happened to them.

Clyde vowed he would constantly try to improve his relationship with Evan. Even when it seemed perfect, he would try to make it better. Would try to keep Evan happy and, if possible, make him even happier. He lifted his head and looked into Evan's eyes. Clyde saw passion there, staring back at him. Sated passion for what they had just done, perhaps, but there was an emotional zeal there as well. Evan liked him more than like, and Clyde knew, Evan would do everything in his power to keep their hold to one another fresh as well.

"You didn't hurt me. It felt great," Evan said. "I never want to hurt you either. Never."

Clyde realized then that he hadn't worn a condom. Everything he had been taught in school and read on his own told him that the unprotected sex they had just experienced with each other was very dangerous. He was confident he had no STD's to pass on to Evan, but wondered if Evan could claim the same thing. He sat up, looked Evan in the eyes. "Are we safe?" he asked.

"What do you mean?" Evan replied.

"We didn't use a condom. I'm pretty sure I'm okay, but..."

"You're right. We should have used something. I've only done that with one other guy, though. We were each other's first. But, just so we both feel safe, we can go to Lewiston to the free clinic and get ourselves tested. It might take a week or two to get the results but, we can get some condoms and use them from now on. Okay?"

"Okay," Clyde said and began to set his head back on Evan's chest when they heard the sudden rumble of John's truck pulling into the driveway. They leapt from the bed, quickly tossed on their clothes and Clyde hurried the bottle of cooking oil back into the kitchen cupboard. He opened the front door and went to the truck to help Mamma into the house. Her skin was pale, a light sweat had risen on her brow from the effort of leaning over her walker, taking one precarious step after another. But, otherwise she looked good considering what she had been through in the last twenty-four hours.

Mamma had lost thirty pounds in the hospital. It wasn't thirty pounds of fat, but fluid. Her heart had been strained with her excessive weight and lack of exercise for years and because it had not been running at full capacity, fluid had built up around her heart and dumped into her extremities. With injections of a diuretic every eight hours, the doctors were able to push the excess fluid from her. Now Mamma could actually fit (just barely) through the door without having to remove it from the frame.

Clyde introduced Evan to Mamma once she was settled into her chair. "Oh. Is this the boy you told me about, John?" she asked.

"Yeah, that's him, Mamma."

"Well, I'm glad you and Clyde hit it off so well. He's a good boy and he needs a good friend like you."

"Thank you, ma'am. Clyde's a great guy. I needed a good friend too. I'm glad we found each other."

"You can thank John. That's the reason he hired you." Mamma pulled her walker closer to her chair, used it to lift herself to her feet. Clyde moved in to help her, but she shushed him away. "I'm fine. Thank you anyway. Mamma's gotta go pee. That damn Lasix they got me on is gonna keep me strapped to the toilet for a while. I'm gonna run a trench in the floor between my chair and the bathroom taking these damned pills."

She started down the hall, then stopped. "Oh, John picked up a few groceries on the way home. They're in the truck. Why don't you bring them in, Clyde. When I come out I'll start cooking. We got chicken, poe-tay-tahs and a nice squash. You staying for sup-pah, Evan?"

"Oh, thank you, Mrs. Chute. but I'm pretty beat. It's been a long week. These guys been running me ragged out in the woods. Can I take a rain check?"

"Dear, you are a friend of Clyde's. You are welcome here anytime you want to come."

"Thank you, ma'am."

"Just call me Mamma. That's what my boys call me and I think, looking at you and Clyde together, you gonna be another son to me. Ayuh, you gonna be together a long time."

Chapter 14
Crossing the Bridge

"Why didn't you want to stay for dinner?" Clyde asked once they were back in Evan's driveway. They were in the Escort, windows rolled down, dust settling on the hood. The car was idling, heat waves rising off the hot metal of the car.

"I wanted to. I want to spend as much time with you as I can. Your mother just came home. She's tired, and I think you need to spend time with your family tonight.

"But you are mine this weekend," Evan continued. "I want you to spend the night with me Saturday. No, actually, I want you to spend the entire weekend with me. I don't care if John needs us to work Sunday. I'll happily work like a dog Sunday because I will have woken next to you that morning. Stay with me Saturday. Stay with me Friday, too. Shit, stay with me every night."

"I think we are going to have a good weekend," Clyde said. He kissed Evan, their lips parted and he pressed his forehead to Evan's. "Oh man, Evan. I don't think I like you more than like, anymore. I think what I'm feeling is off the chart. You make me feel so fucking..." he paused, searched for the right word. "So fucking special. No one has made me feel like you do.

"I am proud with you at my side." Clyde's voice dropped to a whisper as his lips moved closer to Evan's ear. "I'm proud that you want to be with me. I'm proud of myself when I am with you. You make me feel like I am a good man. I must be, to have someone as wonderful as you, want to be with me. But, I want to be a better man for you, because you deserve the best.

"I'm not going to say the L-word though. It's not a bad word like the N-word. In fact, it's a beautiful word. But, I'm not going to say it until I can prove to you that I mean it. I could say it right now and I would know it's true, but that is meaningless unless you know it." Clyde kissed him again, long and slow. Taking the time to feel every curve and groove in Evan's lips with his own. He sighed, heavily. He didn't want today to end. He didn't want to leave, but knew he had to. They would see each other again in less than twelve hours, which was a comfort. But saying good-bye was the hardest thing he ever had to do.

Finally Clyde muttered, "I'll see you in the morning."

Evan slipped from the car. His eyes were wet. "I can hardly wait until the weekend," he said and walked into his home.

"I can hardly wait until tomorrow," Clyde said to himself, then pulled out of the driveway and headed back to John and Mamma.

"So, you get your little boyfriend home alright?" John asked when Clyde stepped back into the trailer. Mamma was in the kitchen, leaning over her walker, mashing potatoes in a large kettle. The trailer smelled of cooked chicken and buttery squash. It made Clyde's mouth water and reminded him of Thanksgiving dinner Mamma cooked each year when his father was still alive. He almost expected to see the Macy's Parade running on the television.

"Yeah, I did. What of it?" Clyde replied. He felt a sudden rush of anger rise up in him. He looked down and noticed his fists flexing and releasing just as John's did when he is mad.

John smiled. "I'm just joking, bud, no need to get defensive."

"I'm not defensive," he said and released his fists. "And I'm not joking either. Evan is my boyfriend."

John froze, a flush of red rose up his neck and turned his face the hot red of arterial blood. "What did you just say?" Clyde had seen that look before. It was the same look on his face as yesterday afternoon when they had their scuffle in the kitchen. It scared him now as much as it did then. But, this was important to him. He needed to tell John the truth. This, like the revelation Clyde discovered about himself yesterday, that Evan was more important to him than that stupid sexual obsession he had for his brother, needed to be brought out into the open air. They needed to talk about this.

"I said, Evan is my boyfriend. I'm gay, John."

John stepped up to him, his face inches from Clyde's. His breath warming Clyde's face. His mouth set in a thin line. John's nostrils flared, like an enraged bull. He was furious, but Clyde didn't care. This was not about John, this was about him. "This is who I am John. This is who I have always been, and always will be. I am gay."

John took a step back. He closed his eyes, counted to three. *One-one thousand, two-one thousand, three-one thousand,* then he opened his eyes and smiled at Clyde. "I know. I've always kind of known."

"No you didn't," Clyde said incredulously.

"Yeah. I did. I knew you were lonely too. I saw it on your face all the time. You were always so sad. That's why I always wanted you to go to Sparky's with me. I figured you might find a nice girl or something. But you never did. So that was why I hired Evan."

"You were playing matchmaker?"

"Yeah. Darlene told me a few weeks ago her cousin had just moved into town and was looking for a job. He was about your age and she thought he might be... ah, well, you know. Like you."

"Gay. It's okay to say it, John," Clyde said, even though the word felt foreign on his own lips as well.

"Yeah, whatever. Anyway, I figured, what the hell? Let's give this a try. You are both guys that like other guys. One dick is just like another so you will probably get together. Maybe that will stop you from moping around here all the time."

"One dick is not like another. Just like one man is not like another. They are all different shapes, sizes."

"Okay, gross," John said. "Look, I'm not going to pretend I understand or like it, but you are my brother. You are a decent guy and if you want to get rammed in the ass, then... well, who really cares?" He bent in closer and whispered so Mamma wouldn't hear from the kitchen, "What I did the other day... well, I'm sorry about that. I'm so sorry. I was mad and I hoped... shit, I hoped it would get you to do this. To come out. A real man lives honestly, and now you are a real man. You are my brother and nothing could make me stop loving you.

"Also," he continued, a light sparkle in his eyes, "I know all you fancy boys want me and I was just fucking with you."

"I guess I proved you wrong," Clyde said. "I didn't touch you so I guess not all us *fancy boys* want you."

"No, you still want me, you just want Evan more. And that's fine by me."

Clyde nodded his head toward the kitchen. "Does Mama know?" he asked.

"Probably. You didn't really hide it all that well. We all saw you mincing around the house."

"I never minced a day in my life."

"Maybe not. Maybe you never sprouted butterfly wings and fluttered around the trailer, but even someone as dim as me knew you were a cock-gobbler from way back."

"You're a jerk," Clyde said and smiled at his brother.

"I know. That's why you love me." He pulled Clyde into his arms and hugged him. "I love you so much, Clyde. You're my favorite brother. I just hope you're happy."

"I am happy. Evan makes me really happy." Clyde realized it was true. For the first time in more than a decade, Clyde could honestly say, he was truly happy.

The cool, clean sheets felt good against Clyde's skin. He looked over Evan, lying in the curl of his arm, head on Clyde's chest. His slow, steady breath ruffled the thin spattering of hair around Clyde's nipples and the patch between. Evan was asleep.

Clyde pulled him closer, hugging Evan to his side a little tighter. He kissed the top of Evan's head, the curly black mop tickling his nose and smelled that strawberry shampoo again. Clyde's hair smelled the same. They had come to Evan's after work, showered together and fell into bed where they finished what was started in the shower.

It was Saturday night and they had just made love. Yes, made love, that is what it was for Clyde. It wasn't fucking or even just sex. There was too much involved to be just sex. It was an intimate, emotional connection that just happened to involve an orgasm.

They hadn't said THE word to each other yet, the L-word. Clyde felt it for Evan and he knew the sentiment was returned, but neither man dared say it. Not yet at least. It had become somewhat of a competition between them. Who would say it first.

John had decided to give everyone Sunday off after all. Before he told Dale and Evan that they did not have to come in Sunday, he consulted with Clyde to make sure it was okay with him. Clyde was now, officially, a decision maker in the business. He quickly agreed, thinking of tonight, of sleeping with Evan in his bed all night. Of holding him in his arms all night.

He was holding Evan, and not just physically. He was also protecting Evan, making sure he had a job with them for as long as he wanted it. Yesterday Clyde called Mr. Wentworth, the man in charge of hiring contracted employees for the mill. He requested a meeting with him. It was set for one day next week. Clyde would inform Wentworth they are expanding the company, had hired two temporary men, but wanted to make them permanent. He planned to request a contract for a larger section of the forest.

If the meeting went well, they could possibly hire even more men, build themselves to level of financial stability neither he or John had ever really known.

And he could still work with Evan every day.

He was taking care of Evan. He was doing what a man did, protect the ones he loved.

Of course Evan was helping Clyde as well. Just by being with him Clyde's confidence was improved. He still wondered if he was worthy of Evan's attentions, in bed and out, but he was working on it. They were working on it together.

Clyde kissed the top of Evan's head again. "I love you," he whispered, sure that Evan was asleep and wouldn't hear him. The competition for the L-word could continue.

Evan's eyes snapped open. "I win," he said, smiling that smile that excited Clyde so.

"You caught me. I said it first though, so I win," Clyde said.

"No. You love me. I'm the winner," Evan said. He kissed Clyde's chest, worked his mouth down over the hard, muscled belly. It still bothered Clyde to be touched like this. He still felt undeserving of the attention. But, Evan enjoyed doing this for him and Clyde liked to see Evan happy. He was beginning to appreciate the sensations of being touched, of lying back and letting Evan explore. It made him want to touch Evan that much more. Evan continued to descend until he was completely under the sheets. "You win too, Clyde. Because, I love you as well."

Then Evan opened his mouth, drew Clyde in and proved it.

Clyde leaned back and let him.

If you enjoyed this story, you can sign up for a free membership at ForbiddenFiction and discuss it with other readers and the author at the *Bridging Obsession* story page at http://forbiddenfiction.com/library/story/PLR-1.000167.

We do our best to proof all our work, but if you spot a text error we missed, please let us know via our website Contact Form at http://forbiddenfiction.com/contact.

About the Author

P.L. Ripley is a born storyteller, weaving worlds since he could first express what he saw in his head. Fascinated with human sexuality, erotic fiction is a natural place for him to explore the connection between sexual excitement and our emotional responses to it. He lives near Bangor, Maine with his partner.

About the Publisher

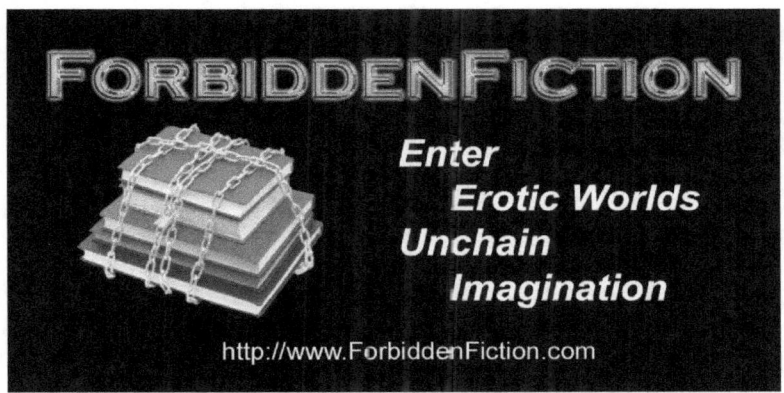

ForbiddenFiction.com is a publisher devoted to writing that breaks the boundaries of original erotic fiction. Our stories combine intense sexuality with quality writing. Stories at ForbiddenFiction.com not only arouse readers through sensations, but also engage them emotionally and mentally through storytelling as well-crafted as the sex is hot.

ForbiddenFiction.com is also designed to be a social reading environment. You'll have fun even if just reading the latest post each day, yet you will have the chance for so much more. Readers and authors can be part of ongoing discussions of specific works and individual authors as well as more general topics.

Sign up for a FREE Membership today at ForbiddenFiction.com